Trichet

by

Carol Preston

PUBLISHED BY WESTVIEW, INC.,

NASHVILLE, TENNESSEE

This book is a work of fiction. Names, characters, places and incidents either are products of the author's imagination or are used fictitiously. Any resemblance to actual events or locales or persons, living or dead, is entirely coincidental.

ISBN 978-1-935271-46-8

First edition, April 2010

PUBLISHED BY WESTVIEW, INC.
P.O. Box 210183
Nashville, Tennessee 37221
www.publishedbywestview.com

Printed in the United States of America on acid free paper.

Acknowledgment:

I wish to thank my friends and family for supporting me, even though it might not be easy. I don't exactly write about fuzzy kittens, butterflies and rainbows. My sincere appreciation especially goes to my two best friends growing up (and your parents, to whom I will always be grateful).

Chapter 1

Cigarette smoke stung Mary's eyes as she quietly studied the people around her. They seemed amused with themselves and their contributions to the various conversations taking place. As usual, her father was drunk, and he was the loudest of the group, interrupting and talking over other people to make his point. His overbearing rudeness dominated the room. At least he hadn't gotten his guitar out yet, which meant it might not be a late night for everyone.

Mary watched her mother smash a cigarette butt into an ashtray that was already full. Small bursts of smoke escaped from her mouth with every word as she leaned forward, talking to a couple of women. One of them laughed as if she had just heard the funniest joke ever. Her coughing seemed to be competing for her laughter as she straightened her inebriated self up in her chair.

Her parents' little get-togethers were all the same, and Mary was tired of this one already. The drunken laughter was so suffocating that she was sure anything would be more fun than being there at that moment. It would be getting dark soon, and Mary knew that's when things began to unravel. They always did. She decided that a little fresh air would help the situation.

She went outside to the front porch and sat down on the squeaky Adirondack chair next to the door. She shifted back and forth in it, liking the noise it made. The chair was used a lot, as it was the only one on the porch, and Mary guessed it was about as broken-in as it could get.

Lying under the chair was her hound dog, Chester. Mary leaned over to get a good look at him. He was a pitiful sight, wagging his tail and peering back at her with pleading eyes. He whined and rolled over onto his back, begging to have his belly scratched. Mary hesitated to touch him, because his fur was wet and muddy and he smelled bad.

"Poor ol' Chester. Buddy, I don't want to pet you too much because you stink," she said, as she rubbed her foot gently against his face. The dog seemed contented with the attention and closed his eyes, resting his head on the cool concrete porch.

The grass was still wet from an earlier rain as Mary stepped into the yard and headed for the barn to see

Tootsie, the only sow left on the farm. She had given birth to nearly a dozen baby pigs several weeks back, most of which had survived the cold nights and the fate of being laid upon and crushed by their mother. Mary had thrown some corn and poured a bucket of water in the pig trough earlier that day. Nevertheless, she wondered if Tootsie might be hungry again.

On the way to the barn, Mary gathered a few handfuls of the wild green onions that were growing in little bunches here and there along the footpath. She was careful to pull them gently so that the onion root stayed intact. Their pungent odor, mixed with the scent of wet dirt, smelled good to her. *No wonder pigs love these things,* she mused, shaking the dirt off of the tiny bulbs.

As Mary got close to the pigpen that extended from the barn, she saw the little pigs running around playing with each other. They were so cute, it was hard to believe they would grow up to be big, rough hogs one day. Climbing over the fence, she greeted the piglets: "Hi, little babies, I got you some wild onions. Come on." They gathered around her as she bent down to pet and feed them. She laughed as they nudged her hands with their snouts, looking for more to eat.

"Here, little piglet," came a voice from behind Mary. She stood up quickly and looked in the direction of the voice. It was one of her daddy's friends who had been in the house just before she walked out. He was red-faced and pudgy. Mary had no idea how old the man was, but he seemed a bit younger than her parents. Sweat rolled down the sides of his face, which he absentmindedly wiped away.

Leaning against the fence post, he was smiling at her in a way that made her feel nervous. He looked downright smug as his beady, deep-set eyes took in the sight of her. "Sooweee!" he called out with his hand cupped around his mouth, but he wasn't looking at the pigs. He was staring at her instead.

As Mary backed away from the fence, her shoe got stuck in the mud and came off her foot. She bent over to retrieve it, almost losing her balance. Once she righted herself, she looked up to see the man glance around to see if anyone else was coming. His beady little eyes then focused back on her. He seemed amused at Mary's clumsiness, and it made her feel self-conscious. She felt her face getting flushed.

"Are these your little pigs, honey?" the man asked, sounding sickeningly-sweet. Again he looked over his shoulder, as though assessing whether or not anyone could see him. He seemed satisfied that no one could and settled back into conversation. "How old are you getting to be now?"

Mary pretended to be more interested in the pigs than in what the man was saying. Without looking up, she answered, "I'm twelve."

The man leaned toward Mary and spoke in a hushed tone, as if he were going to share a secret with her, "Well, you're getting to be a big girl, ain't ya?"

Mary shrugged.

"You better come on out of that pigpen, honey, because a mama pig don't like nobody to be around her babies. She might try to bite you."

She looked at his ugly face. "I ain't scared. I've been in here a bunch of times. That big mama pig just ignores me."

He stood up straight. "Now, come on out of there, girl. You're gonna get worms from walking around in that pig mess. Come on out here with me." He motioned with his hand, obviously annoyed at her resistance.

"No, really, I don't want to." Mary felt trapped, and looked past the man to see if anybody else was walking around the house.

"Come on, baby. Come to me." The man leaned over the fence toward her, to be as close as possible without actually climbing over it. "I want a hug. Want to give me a hug, little piglet?" He sat his beer on the fencepost and stretched his arms out toward her, careful not to touch his shirt to the dirty fence.

His smile, which didn't quite reach his hard little eyes, made Mary feel sick. She stood still, not really knowing what to do next. *What if he comes into this pen after me?* She considered whether or not running into the barn would be the best thing to do.

After impatiently standing by the fence for a few minutes, the man shook his head and finished his beer. Throwing his empty beer can toward the barn he muttered, "I'll get you one of these days, little piglet." As he walked toward the house, he looked back over his shoulder at Mary. She hadn't moved from her spot in the pigpen.

Mary sat down on the side of the trough, relieved. She didn't want to go back to the house for a while, because that man would surely be there. Besides, she didn't like it when everybody was drunk and acting silly. "I'd rather be with a hundred pigs than that stupid bunch," she said to herself, scratching behind one of the baby pigs' ears.

As Mary watched the little pigs run around after each other, she sadly realized that she didn't really have a lot of friends. She thought about all the animals on the farm: a sow and her babies, a few ducks, a dog and two cats. It was hardly a farm — more of a dismal piece of land where a few animals were lucky to have any shelter at all, let alone food to eat. But Mary liked to think of it as a farm, and for now those animals seemed as miserable as she, and at least they had each other.

Mary climbed out of the pigpen and went into the barn. It was fascinating to her and one of her favorite places to spend time. Especially the loft. Besides being a good vantage point to the house, there were always lots of spiders and empty, dried dirt dauber tubes up there. She liked to poke at them with a stick and watch them crumble.

Besides the loft, there were four stalls in the barn. The rough-sawn doors on each stall were attached with rusty, over-sized hinges that had stood the test of time. A handmade latch had been made for each door out of a rectangular block of wood screwed to the door facing which was simply turned horizontally to keep it closed.

The barn was used mostly for the storage of junk. Things were piled in three of the stalls, including broken-down furniture, antiquated farm implements that Mary was sure no one would ever use again, and an old saddle that was covered with a thick layer of dust and spider webs. Mary had considered digging the saddle out to clean it up, but it was covered in spider egg sacks which she pictured popping open, allowing hundreds of baby spiders to escape and bite her all over.

One of the stalls at the front of the barn was used for the pigs. A rough opening that her daddy had cut in the side of the barn allowed them to come and go from the stall to the fenced-in pen. Tootsie often scratched her backside on the uneven boards as she exited the barn. It was a sight, and it always made Mary laugh.

Mary also thought it was funny to see Tootsie go inside and lie down. She always looked exhausted, like she just couldn't stand up anymore, practically collapsing on piled up hay to go to sleep. Then she let out a huge sigh, as if she were completely spent.

From the loft, Mary could see the cars that were still parked at the house and monitor who had left. She wasn't even sure what car that beady-eyed man drove, so she figured she'd wait until most of them were gone before she went back. Mary wasn't so good at waiting. She wished she had paid more attention to what people were driving.

As she sat and watched the house, smelling the mustiness of the barn, memories of hiding there over the years came to her. That time she had a loose tooth that her mother had threatened to pull, other times when she had gotten in trouble for something, and lots of times when she just wanted to be alone.

One of the cats was in the loft with her, lying on an old horse blanket that someone had stored there. Mary yawned and rested her head on the blanket next to the cat. She remembered her mother telling her she didn't look well that morning. Mary admitted to herself that she did indeed feel achy and exhausted. *Maybe she knows me better than I knew myself.*

"Hey, Striped Britches. Good kitty," Mary said as she rubbed the cat's head. He half-heartedly reached out to tap her on the nose with his paw before laying his head back down. Mary rubbed her legs together to satisfy a lingering itch from some mosquito bites. Listening to the cat purr, she fell asleep quickly. She dreamt about the man who wanted to hug her. He was drunk and kissing her all over her face. She was paralyzed and could do nothing to stop him.

Chapter 2

When she saw a girl walking down the road toward her house, Mary threw down the stick with which she was drawing in the dirt. *Who in the world is that?* she wondered.

Mary curiously watched the girl as she came down the driveway and approached her. She had long, blonde hair that was tied back with a ribbon. At a loss for words, Mary caught herself gawking at her.

The girl smiled big, and Mary noticed how white and straight her teeth were. She was about Mary's size, but she looked a little younger. Cute and small, the little girl moved gracefully but purposefully.

Mary was slightly intimidated by her immediate friendliness and debated on whether to smile back at her or yell hello. By the time she decided, the girl was already too close to her for yelling, so she managed a grin.

"Hi, I'm Melanie," the girl said when she got close enough. "I just moved into the house next door." She pointed toward where she lived.

"The yellow house with the porch swing?"

"Yeah."

"I'm Mary."

The girls stood awkwardly, looking at each other expectantly. Mary spoke again: "I'm twelve years old. How old are you?"

"I just turned eleven," Melanie answered.

Mary nodded, but couldn't think of anything to say except, "Oh."

Melanie looked a little disappointed, as if she had anticipated a different response. After a long pause, she asked, "So, maybe you can come over and play at my house sometime?"

"Yes, I would really like to." Mary sized Melanie up. She assumed the girl had moved from town, because she was wearing fingernail polish and smelled like perfume. She was wearing purple corduroy overalls with a lacy T-shirt underneath. Mary was in awe of the girl's prettiness, which seemed out of place somehow.

Mary looked down at her own clothes –– rolled-up jeans and a shirt that was at least one size too small. Her fingernails had dirt crammed underneath them.

Embarrassed, she hid her hands behind her back, hoping they wouldn't be noticed.

Melanie casually observed Mary's house and yard. As she looked around, Mary followed her gaze, wondering what she was thinking. The house was rather plain-looking, with clapboard siding, a concrete porch and handmade shutters. On the smallish side, it was not in the best shape, but Mary thought it looked good enough.

Mary decided to spare Melanie the story about moving into the house. She remembered moving in when she was three years old. It was basically a two-room shack onto which her father had built three bedrooms soon after moving in. To his credit, somehow he incorporated the old part of the house with the newer part fairly well.

She recalled that the day they moved into the house that there was an old lady living in it who refused to move out. She still believed it was hers, refusing to leave even as Mary's family was moving their things into it. Mary wondered how her parents ever got that lady out of the place and where she'd gone. After pondering the old lady's plight for a moment, Mary turned her attention once again to Melanie, who was still taking everything in with a curious look on her face.

The house backed up to an empty field that had a creek running through it. Behind the creek, thick woods covered a hill, beyond which nothing else was visible from their standpoint. Mary had always wanted to climb the hill to see what was on the other side of it, but she backed out every time for fear of the unknown. "I'm kind of scared of Bigfoot, so I don't go back there in those woods." Mary's attempt at being funny made Melanie look at her skeptically. "Never mind, I was just kidding."

"What's that?" Melanie asked, pointing to the well house that sat in the yard.

"You never saw a well house before? It's there to cover the water well and pump. See, Daddy made it look like the house," she said, pointing out that it had the same clapboard siding on it.

Next to the well house was a makeshift patio made of concrete that looked like it was left over from some other project and just dumped on the ground. A couple of big trees, about ten feet apart, shaded the area.

Beyond the two shade trees, there was a worn footpath that led from the house to the barn. Numerous small mud puddles filled ruts in the footpath, which was otherwise dry.

The barn wasn't very impressive. Leaning back as if it was too tired to stand up straight, it looked practically useless. Part of its rusty tin roof was missing, and some of it was curiously bent over from the wind, folded on top of itself.

"You like our old barn?" Mary laughed when she saw Melanie's reaction to it.

"Do you still use it?" Melanie answered, eyebrows raised.

"Yeah, we have some pigs in it. Daddy says the boards are so warped and far apart you could throw a good-sized cat clear through it."

Melanie put her hand over her mouth and giggled.

Along the footpath was an outhouse, standing with the door wide open. Mary noticed Melanie studying it, trying to figure out what it was. "That's just an old outhouse," she said after a minute.

Melanie looked puzzled.

"We have a bathroom in the house now, but that's where we had to go before the bathroom was built." Mary suddenly felt embarrassed about it. She hadn't given it much thought before, even though most people didn't have outhouses anymore.

"Oh." Melanie changed the subject. "Well, why don't you come over to my house later this afternoon? My mama picked some strawberries, and when you dip them in sugar, they are so good." She licked her lips for effect.

Mary smiled. "Okay, I'll come over later, then." She watched Melanie leave and felt excited about having a new friend.

Later that afternoon, Mary combed her hair and changed her clothes. She was going to Melanie's house, and she wanted to look nice. Looking in the mirror at herself, she saw a skinny girl with long, stringy brown hair. She liked her green eyes, but hated her crooked teeth and freckles. After snapping a barrette in her hair, she thought she looked okay to meet Melanie's mother.

When she got to Melanie's house, Mary knocked on the door and heard what sounded like dogs inside, their nails scratching against the floor and their name tags tinkling as they approached the front door. Mary backed away a little, in case they decided to jump on her when the door opened. She knew that not all dogs were like Chester -- too timid to make himself a nuisance to people.

"Don't worry, they won't bite you. I'm Melanie's mom." The lady smiled and welcomed Mary into the house as two large black labs pushed past her and ran out into the yard. Mary was impressed with the inside dogs. She was never allowed to have a dog in the house, and it surprised her that they could be so clean and shiny. She wondered how Chester would look, all cleaned up. *Nope, there's no way that old hound dog would ever let me do that to him,* she concluded.

The inside of the house was unlike what Mary was used to seeing. It was cozy-looking, with mismatched, yet fancy pieces of furniture. It smelled nice, and there were lit candles sitting here and there. Mary supposed it must be an elegant thing to have candles burning in the broad daylight.

There were lots of records and a record player on a bookshelf that spanned an entire wall of the living room.

Mary noticed a John Denver album on one of the shelves that hadn't made its way back into its jacket yet.

Family pictures, sitting just about everywhere, seemed to be smiling at her. They looked like such friendly people. Without even realizing it, Mary was smiling back at them. Her family didn't even own a camera, she realized. She made a mental note to ask her mother about that fact when she got home. After all, she didn't have a single picture of Chester, and she really wished that she did.

The kitchen was a happy-looking room with rays of sunshine coming through the window that settled on the kitchen table. It looked like a warm spotlight, shining brilliantly through dainty, white eyelet curtains.

Mary noticed how clean everything was and felt slightly envious that Melanie had such a lovely place to live, but she was grateful that it was being shared with her. The warmth and serenity of it were palpable. Mary was certain that she would be spending as much time as possible at Melanie's house.

It even had a smell that she couldn't place, but it was something familiar. Something like a mixture of food, detergent, the dogs, fake greenery, so many things at once. It smelled like home.

After eating a bowl of strawberries with sugar, the girls were ushered outside by Melanie's mother. "You girls go play for a while," she said with a wink. She was the prettiest lady Mary had ever seen. It was obvious where Melanie had gotten her good looks and personality. Kindness seemed to radiate from her, and Mary realized she loved her already.

"Who is that?" Melanie asked, as an old man in overalls walked down the road in front of the house. Sitting on the front porch swing, her foot lazily pushed against the porch to move the swing occasionally. Mary was sitting next to her, relaxed, knees pulled up to her chest. She followed Melanie's gaze to see who she was talking about.

"That's just an old man who lives in that house up there." Mary nodded toward a dilapidated shack that sat on a small hill across the road.

"I didn't know anybody lived up there in that old place. It looks like it's going to fall down or something," Melanie said, shaking her head with wonder.

"Would you believe that used to be a schoolhouse?"

"No. Really?" Melanie seemed astonished at this news.

"Yeah. I don't know what the old man's name is, but everybody calls him Doc. He ain't no doctor, though. That's for sure." Melanie laughed at Mary's comment. "Seriously, though, he's got something wrong with him. He can't talk plain."

"Why is he staring at us like that?" Melanie asked, watching Doc suspiciously.

"He might be retarded, too, I don't know," Mary answered dismissively. "He comes down to the house sometimes to give my mama stuff from his garden, but I just run off and do something else because I don't like him. He calls me 'Trichet'."

"What does that mean?"

"Mama says he's trying to call me Cricket, but it comes out as 'Trichet'."

Melanie laughed. "That's funny."

"You ought to hear the other stuff he says. We can't figure out what he's saying half the time."

"Well, he makes me nervous peeping around with his hands in his pockets. I can see why you don't like him."

"Watch out for him, because he likes to put his hands on your boobies."

Melanie raised her eyebrows and instinctively covered her chest with her hands.

"That's right. He'll give you a sucker, then pretend he wants to hug you. Only he hugs you from behind and tries to feel of your boobies."

Melanie looked mortified, and Mary was satisfied that she was able to get such a rise out of her new friend.

Chapter 3

"The pump is burned up. You're gonna have to get it replaced," the bald repairman said as he stepped down the ladder from the well house onto the crude concrete patio. He was shaking his head as he wiped his hands on a tattered bandana. "That's gonna cost you."

"Dammit. Well, I don't have any money right now, so it'll have to wait. I guess we'll just have to make do." Robert spat on the concrete as he took off his blue flannel shirt and draped it over the ladder. The T-shirt he'd been wearing underneath it had sweat stains under the arms. Mary crinkled her nose at the sight of it.

Robert turned to his wife. "Judy, get as many milk jugs for drinking water as you can, and we'll get them filled up at the neighbor's house. And I reckon we'll have to take baths in the creek."

"Oh, are you kidding me? Again?" Judy sighed as she walked toward the house. "Hauling milk jugs of water. . ." Judy was oblivious to Mary standing by until she nearly bumped into her. Mary moved to avoid a collision. Judy looked at her as if seeing her for the first time.

"Mary, your daddy says we won't have water for a while, so you'll need to take baths at a friend's house or something. If it ain't the well drying up over the summer or the pipes freezing in the winter, it's the damned pump breaking." Sighing and muttering, she pulled open the squeaky screen door, displacing a sleeping cat.

Mary watched her mother walk into the house and felt her disappointment. It was always a hardship when there was no water in the house. Walking behind Judy, Mary caught up to her and said, "Mama?"

Judy turned around quickly. "What?" She frowned at Mary, waiting for a response.

"Uh, I was going to ask if I could go stay with Melanie tonight."

"Who? Yes, yes, just go somewhere." Judy waved Mary away as if she couldn't stand the sight of her.

"Mama, why are you so mad at me all the time?" Mary said, her feelings raw, causing her voice to come out weird and high-pitched. Why she chose to confront her mother about it, she didn't know. She braced herself for a nasty retort.

Judy took a deep breath and answered, "No water, plus the fact that the only heat we have in the winter is a fireplace and there's no air conditioning in the summer. . . It makes this house downright unlivable sometimes. I don't know what in the world made us move out here to this shithole so far out in the country."

Mary looked at her sympathetically, but she didn't know what to say. She was actually relieved that the conversation hadn't escalated to a smack in the face.

"I'm sorry, I didn't mean to be so rough with you, but right now, I'm pissed," Judy said, fanning herself with her hand. "Just leave me alone for a while, okay?"

Mary went back outside to get away from her mother. She walked over to the well house to ask her father if she could go to her friend's house for the night, but he was still talking to the man who had come to look at the pump and didn't acknowledge her presence.

"I'll call you when I come up with the money to get this thing fixed, all right, buddy?" Robert said, handing the man some money for his time. He looked at the few dollars he had been given, shook his head in disappointment, and left.

Robert opened a beer and kicked the well house, cursing. He leaned against a tree. "Shit. I need to make some goddamned money," he grumbled as he turned his beer up to finish it off in one final gulp. He burped and threw the can across the yard, looking disgusted.

Chester raised his head momentarily to see what was going on. He yawned, stretched, then apathetically laid back down and closed his eyes. *Even the dog has gotten weary of this place,* Mary thought.

She could see that it was going to be a bad night at home and decided it was time to go to Melanie's house. She started walking up the road without telling her parents. Why bother? She wouldn't be missed, and she knew it. Still, she couldn't resist looking back at the house to see if anyone had noticed that she was leaving. Apparently, they hadn't.

Not being missed had its good points. The best part about it was that she had all the freedom in the world. Sometimes that felt good, and she pretended she was grown and could come and go as she pleased. She even rubbed it in to Melanie a few times that she didn't have to ask permission to go see her. But that didn't change the fact that mostly she felt absolutely forsaken, like no one even cared. *It's just not fair,* Mary thought, as she fought back tears of frustration.

It had gotten foggy, and the air felt damp. Mary pulled her jacket around her and daydreamed about summer as she walked to Melanie's house. Buttercups had broken through the ground, practically overnight, and Mary considered picking some from the side of the road to give to Melanie's mother.

Ahead, she could see a figure walking toward her on the opposite side of the road. As the person got closer, Mary realized it was Doc. She wanted to look straight ahead and ignore him, but she couldn't help but take a sideways glance at him. He was smiling at her as he passed her, his shiny gums revealing his lack of teeth.

As usual, Doc's hands were jammed into the pockets of his overalls. Mary wondered if that was why his back was so humped over, from keeping his hands in his pockets all the time. His walk reminded her of Frankenstein, with his heavy, flat footsteps. He seemed to be braced against the wind, with his shoulders all stooped over and his eyes squinty.

A watch in one of the little bib pockets of his overalls was attached to a chain that looped around to one of the fasteners, swaying back and forth as he walked. As he approached Mary, she could tell he was going to say something. His eyes focused on her; she tried to look away, but she couldn't.

"Trichet," he said in a hoarse, low voice as he nodded to her. A provocative smile danced on his lips as he watched her reaction. Mary quickly looked down at the ground and started walking faster toward Melanie's house.

"That old man gives me the creeps, Melanie!" Mary said as she sat down on the porch swing with her friend. She faked a shudder for effect.

"Yeah, he's creepy and gross all right. My mama told me to stay away from him, and if I see him to go the other way."

"I think he thinks he's sexy or something," Mary said in a whisper, leaning toward her friend.

"Oh, stop it!" Melanie said, laughing hard.

"You should've seen the way he was smiling at me when he called me 'Trichet'."

"No, that's something I don't want to see." Melanie made a disgusted face. "Yuck."

Feeling confident enough of this new friendship to come right out and ask for a favor, Mary said, "Mel, I hate to ask, but. . ."

"What?"

"Well, can I spend the night with you? We don't have any water at home, and Daddy's already getting drunk." At this point, she didn't even care if Melanie knew how pathetic her home life was.

"Oh, yeah! Of course you can. I didn't know what the heck you were about to ask after that story about Doc." Melanie laughed. "You know I'm just kidding. You can stay here any time you want to."

"Are you sure your mother won't mind?"

"Of course not! Hey, we can have pizza for dinner!" Melanie clapped her hands with excitement.

Relieved, Mary smiled and felt like hugging Melanie, but she just said thank you instead. Melanie's generosity and friendliness seemed to be effortless, and Mary marveled at the way she stayed positive about everything. She hoped it would rub off on her. Meanwhile, she basked in the affection she felt for the girl.

One of Melanie's dogs even seemed to be welcoming Mary as he walked up and put his paw on her leg. The dog had an expressive face; his eyebrows going up and down made Mary laugh.

"Your dog is smart," Mary said as she rubbed the dog's head. "My dog Chester stinks all the time, but he's sweet. I think he's pretty smart, too. He barks like this when he's on the trail of a rabbit: 'bowww bowww!'"

Melanie smiled. "You're funny. And you know what? I'm pretty sure you're going to be my new best friend."

Mary's very soul was lifted by Melanie's words. She could tell the words were genuine and heartfelt. "You are definitely my best friend."

Before going to sleep that night, Mary said a silent prayer. She was thankful to find someone so wonderful to be with, and she prayed for many more days of fun with her new friend.

Chapter 4

"You won't believe this, but my parents are going to run a beer joint," Mary told Melanie when she met her at the creek, a new habit the girls had gotten into once they realized how nice it was to be alone together. They found that they could talk about anything there and not be shushed by Melanie's mother for talking too loud or too dirty.

As she waited for a response from Melanie, Mary gazed at the water. It sparkled from the sunlight that filtered through the leaves of the trees. The delayed reaction from her friend made her feel as if her words had washed right down the creek with the current.

"Did you hear what I said?" Mary asked.

"What? Yeah, I heard you," Melanie answered as she balanced her weight on slippery rocks in the creek. "That's all they need is more beer. What they really need is some food in the house." She teetered from one rock to another, seemingly unconcerned about the water seeping into her canvas shoes.

Mary had bent down to look for flat rocks to skip across the creek. She stopped for a moment to think about what Melanie had said. It almost seemed insulting, even though Mary knew that Melanie was right. It felt bad to hear someone say something negative about her parents, even if it was the truth, and she felt surprisingly defensive about it.

"Yeah, I guess you're right about that, except sometimes we have stuff out of the garden to eat," Mary answered, feeling the need to take up for her parents. Somehow, they just seemed to have a harder time of things than most people, whether their problems were self-imposed or not. "It's probably not as bad as it sounds, though. It's not like we're starving or something."

Melanie shrugged.

"Anyway, about the beer joint. . .it should be fun, because they told me that there are arcade games in there. And they said I can go sometimes and play." Mary hoped her last statement would make her friend jealous, or at the very least sorry that she had acted so indifferently.

It worked. Melanie looked at Mary, wide-eyed, and smiled. "Can I go over there and play, too? I mean, wouldn't it be fun if we could both go over there? I've never been in a place like that before."

"Oh, yeah, it'll be a blast!" Mary wasn't sure she was telling the truth. She didn't know if Melanie would be allowed to go, but it was fun to talk about, anyway.

The girls sat together on the edge of the creek and watched minnows darting around in the water. It felt good that day, the sun beating down, warming their backs. A toad was groaning somewhere and the wind had picked up a little. Melanie walked into the water a couple of feet to get a good look at what she thought was a baby snake. It turned out to be a stick.

"I guess I need to get on home," Mary said, looking toward the direction of her house. She wanted to stall a few more minutes to be with her friend, but she couldn't think of anything else to say.

"But you just got here," whined Melanie as she walked on her tippy-toes out of the creek and sat cross-legged on the ground.

"Yeah, I know, but I'm supposed to go with my parents to carry some supplies to the bar. Tonight's their first night to start managing it, and I guess we have to set up stuff before people show up."

"What kind of stuff?"

"I don't exactly know. Just stuff."

"Hmmm," Melanie answered. She absentmindedly watched a bunch of leaves and dust in the distance, blowing around in a circle. It looked like a miniature tornado. Mary looked at it, too, momentarily mesmerized by it.

"Hmmm, what?" she asked finally.

"I suppose y'all need to get all the booze ready for the drunks," Melanie said, still focused on the whirling leaves.

Mary felt like her friend was being derogatory toward her, but she brushed it off because she figured Melanie was probably just trying to be funny. Besides, it wasn't worth arguing over. "I guess so. I'll talk to you later tonight."

Melanie seemed to sense that she had been too cavalier. "Yeah, call me when you get home. I want to hear all about that place." She smiled at Mary.

"Thanks, Mel. I will." Mary breathed a sigh of relief. For a minute, she thought her friend had stopped caring about her. It dawned on her, then, how much value she had given to Melanie's opinion.

Later that afternoon, with Judy and Mary behind him carrying plastic cups and a big bag of supplies, Robert unlocked the door to the bar. It was covered with a thick coat of black paint which was chipping off, leaving a mess on the steps leading up to it.

From the road, Mary had never thought the place looked that bad, but seeing it up close changed her mind. It was unkempt, and without the usual multitude of cars that were parked around the building at night, the deserted appearance of it was depressing.

The bar had a nasty reputation around town, one that Mary had heard about for a long time. She had often wondered what it was like inside. She imagined bar fights like she'd seen on television –– people hitting each other with beer bottles, loose women dancing on the tables. The sordid visions that filled her head when she had thought about it made her apprehensive to go inside. She almost expected a wild scene awaiting her there, as if it were non-stop, around-the-clock bedlam.

As they stepped inside Mary stumbled, almost dropping the stack of cups she was carrying. It was dark inside the bar, belying the fact that it was still sunny outside. It took a moment for Mary's eyes to adjust to the contrast. She thought this must be what it was like to walk into a cave. . . a dank, smelly cave. The place had an odor of stale beer, cigarettes, and armpits. And it was eerily quiet. Somehow, Mary was thrown off by the feel of it, almost like a déjà vu experience.

Judy turned on the lights and took the items she was carrying behind the bar. She began putting things away, whistling as she worked. Mary couldn't remember a time when she had heard her mother do that, and it seemed sort of pleasant -- off-key and resonant in the stinky void of a place.

Robert immediately went to the beer cooler and got a beer for himself, then began to take stock of what he needed to do before opening later that evening. From somewhere he had produced a checklist, which he placed on the bar and studied in between gulps of beer. He seemed pleased with this newfound charge as barkeeper.

Mary looked around, taking in the layout of what appeared to be just one big room that had been partitioned off in sections as needed. As simple as it was, it made sense, and Mary thought it seemed like a good use of space. Even the illuminated beer logo clock, placed strategically amidst the tacky décor, seemed practical.

The bar itself had eight stools scooted up to it. Mary noted that it looked cleaner than anything else she had seen so far. The top of the bar was downright shiny, in fact. Empty ashtrays were stacked neatly at the end of it, next to a plastic bowl filled with matchbooks.

Adjacent to the bar was an area of about a dozen tables with all kinds of mismatched chairs, which had been placed upside down on top of them. An empty ashtray also sat on each table. She hoped she would never be the one in charge of cleaning them out, but she suspected she might be.

There was a small dance floor with a juke box lit up in the corner, separated from the rest of the bar by a knee-wall with support posts at each end. The dance floor, made of hardwood, looked worn and filthy. Mary noticed dark spots on the floors, and wondered what they were and how they had gotten there. She figured whatever it was, it probably wasn't good.

Against the wall, toward the bathrooms, there were two arcade games and a poker game machine. They were going through their demonstration cycles, lights blinking and fake points racking up on the screen. Mary stared at the games with a smile. She immediately wished Melanie was there with her.

Her mother, apparently noticing Mary staring at the games, said, "Now, you can't be here when the bar is open. It's against the law for you to be here when people are drinking."

"That's fine with me," Mary answered, "anyways, I don't like to be around drunk people and cigarette smoke."

Judy seemed to catch herself frowning, and pasted a sarcastic-looking smile on her face. "I know you don't. Wouldn't want a little princess like you to be around such awful things."

Judy's mocking tone didn't escape Mary, and she struggled to figure out why her mother seemed to be so defensive with her all the time. She wondered at what level she'd need to stoop so that her mother wouldn't accuse her of acting like she's better than everybody else. Maybe she should get knocked up by some lazy, low-class jackass from out in the holler? Move into a junky trailer parked in a field somewhere? Become a helpless, hopeless sorry excuse for a person and take up self-loathing? Mary decided that if that's what it would take, no thank you, she wasn't that desperate to prove herself worthy of anything.

Chapter 5

"Daddy just brought me home. Now he's going back to that stinking rat-hole," Mary said to Melanie over the phone, as she closed the door behind her and watched her father drive away. "Ah, sweet freedom. It's good to be home. Alone."

"Good. You don't need to be at that place," Melanie said with a yawn.

"What're you doing now?" Mary asked, yawning in sympathy.

"I'm watching *Love Boat*."

"Oh yeah, I'll watch it, too. Well, I guess I should say I'll *try* to watch it. The screen on the TV keeps rolling, so I have to smack it really hard on the top so it'll be still long enough to watch the stupid thing."

"Oh, that's funny. Maybe y'all need a new one."

"Yeah, right. Lord only knows how old this one is. Hell, it's amazing we have a phone over here."

"Hey, did your daddy fix the well? Do you have water now?" asked Melanie, sounding distracted. Mary figured she was probably more interested in watching the TV show than talking on the phone.

"Yes, finally. Would you believe my daddy took a bath in the creek the other day?"

Melanie laughed. "That's pretty funny."

"Yeah. Well, I'm going to fix me something to eat. Want me to call you back later?"

"If you want to, that's fine. I'm going to brush my teeth and go lay in the bed."

Mary thought Melanie sounded distant, which seemed to have become a trend with her. She tried to figure out what she might have said or done to make her friend back away from her. It could be that they were just growing apart. The thought of that happening literally made Mary's chest tighten with worry.

After hanging up the phone, Mary opened the freezer to find something to eat. *Mel's right*, she thought, *we really don't have much food around here.* She found a frozen dinner, and she set it on the counter to be cooked. Before she had a chance to turn on the oven, she heard Chester barking outside.

Mary walked to the front door and looked out the window into the darkness. Just then the phone rang, and it made her jump. *That must be Melanie again,* she thought as she ran to answer it, sliding expertly with her stocking feet across the linoleum floor. "Hello?"

"You ever been fucked?" said a man's husky voice, barely above a whisper. For a second, Mary wasn't sure what she had just heard. She stood motionless, listening; he said nothing more. She strained to listen for background noises on the phone, but it sounded like dead air. *Maybe he hung up,* she thought. She softly placed the phone on its cradle and stared at it, feeling shaky.

It rang again, and she answered.

"You been fuckin' them boys again, ain't ya?" the voice said. It didn't sound familiar to Mary, but she couldn't swear to it. She listened intently, hoping for a hint of recognition. "Who is this?" she asked after a minute, in as grown-up a voice as she could muster. She didn't want to sound afraid. Twisting the phone cord around her fingers, she listened closely, anxiously awaiting something recognizable that she could identify.

"I know you been fuckin' them boys. You better tell me the truth."

Mary couldn't believe what the man was saying. Who could this be? "No," she answered firmly. She couldn't think of anything else to say. There was silence on the line. She detected a slight breathing noise, but it was nearly inaudible, and she wondered if it was just the echo of her own breathing. She felt compelled to speak up and be rude to the man.

"Who is this, anyway?" she snapped. "You're probably calling people out of the phone book. You don't even know who I am." She was breathless as she waited for his response.

"If you don't tell the truth, I'll tell your daddy. . ." His voice trailed off, making him difficult to hear.

"What did you say?"

"You heard what I said. I'll tell your daddy. And you're gonna get in so much trouble."

"You don't even know who my daddy is, and you're crazy!" Mary yelled into the phone before hanging up. She was scared now. *What if this person really does know who I am and where I live, and what if he knows that I'm here alone!*

She chewed her nails and paced. *I'll call Daddy at the bar and tell him,* she decided. As she reached to pick up the phone, it rang again. This time she picked it up without saying anything.

"I *do* know who your daddy is, and I'll tell him. I'll tell Robert."

Mary immediately hung up the phone and ran to make sure both the front and back doors were locked. They were. Then she ran back to the phone and called the bar. It rang at least a dozen times before her father finally answered.

"Daddy, some man is calling and he's saying some really nasty things over the phone." She took a deep, shaky breath and continued, "Bad words and dirty talk. He knows who you are, and he knows where we live. I'm really scared!"

"Wait a minute. Did he threaten you? Hold on." The phone went silent for a moment. "Here's your mother."

"Mary, this is Mama. Robert's coming home right now to get you, okay? Stay on the phone with me, honey, and you'll be all right. Are the doors locked?"

"Yes, and Chester stopped barking, so I think I'm okay here."

"The dog was barking? At what?"

"I don't know."

"Who is it, Mary, do you know?"

"No, I didn't recognize the voice."

"What did he say to you?"

"Well, uh. . . He asked me if I've ever been fucked," Mary stammered, choking on her own words. She'd never said a dirty word like that in front of her mother, and she felt ashamed. She started crying.

"It'll be okay, honey, your daddy will be there in a minute," Judy said, sounding concerned. Mary was relieved that her mother was being so kind. She was trembling so much that her teeth were chattering.

There was a pause. "Mary, I have to take some money up here at the bar. I'm going to put you on the phone with Devin –– he just walked in the door. Stay on the phone with him until your daddy gets there." Mary heard her mother talking in a muffled tone as if her hand were over the mouthpiece. "Here he is."

"Hey, little girl, you okay?" said Devin. Mary liked Devin. In fact, she had a crush on him, which her mother had teased her about before. "Some bad man saying some nasty things to you on the phone? Don't worry, honey, your daddy's going to be there in a minute. You just stay on the phone with me."

"Okay." Mary felt tongue-tied and wasn't sure what to say to him. She hoped her father would be home soon.

"So, what're you doing tonight, little darlin'?" Devin asked. "Watching TV?"

Mary nodded, momentarily oblivious to the fact that he couldn't hear her, then she answered, "Yes, I was. I'm really okay, just scared is all."

"You're gonna be alright. Just let me know when your daddy gets there. I'm right here with you, Sugar."

Mary saw headlights coming down the driveway. She anxiously watched them until she could confirm that it was her daddy's car. "Okay, Daddy's here. I'm fine now."

"So, you comin' to the bar with your daddy?" Devin asked, in the sexiest voice Mary had ever heard.

"Um, uh, I didn't think about that," she admitted. "I don't know. I guess so."

"Well, to be on the safe side, I think you better do that. Tell your daddy you want to be with your mama. He'll make sure you're safe in her arms, okay?"

"Okay. Bye." Mary hung up the phone and went to sit on the couch next to the front door. She turned around to look out the window and watched her father get out of the car.

Robert stood in the driveway looking around, listening, studying the darkness for something. He had a worried look on his face when he unlocked the door and came into the house. He hadn't been drinking, and for that Mary was thankful. He came in and sat on the couch with her, and she started crying again.

"I know that was scary. I don't know who that was, but if I ever find him, I'll kill him," Robert vowed as he patted his daughter's back. "Some son-of-a-bitch that can't leave young girls alone. He needs to be shot."

"What are we going to do?" Mary asked, wiping her face with her shirt sleeve.

"Well, I don't know. But tonight, I have to get back to the bar. You can come with me. At least you'll be safe there. But we have to keep you hidden, because you're not supposed to be there."

Chapter 6

Once they got to the bar and stepped inside, Mary's eyes quickly adjusted to the smoky darkness. The noise and smell of the place were equally as loud as she looked around for a familiar face. She saw a few people that she thought she knew, though she wasn't sure if she could remember their names.

Lined up at the bar were several men who looked her over appreciatively as she studied the crowd. It made her feel creepy. There were a few women in the bar, but they barely glanced at her. She suddenly wished that she could leave. The place smelled like stale beer and puke.

Judy stepped from behind the bar and motioned to Mary. "Come on back here with me."

There was a barstool sitting behind the bar that couldn't be seen from the front door. Mary could still see the guys who were sitting at the bar, but the people sitting at the tables weren't visible to her. She hopped up on the stool, noting that the legs were uneven and wobbled when she shifted positions. *There's not a dang thing about this place that's any count.* She focused on a little black and white television that was sitting behind the bar. The picture was so snowy she couldn't make out what was on.

A man at the bar nodded and smiled at her. When she didn't smile back, he frowned and took a drink of his beer. *He's actually pouting,* Mary thought in amazement. *And he's a grown man, too. I guess men never get too old to act stupid.* The man drummed his fingers on the bar for a couple of minutes then got up to go to the bathroom.

On the tiny dance floor, a few people were attempting to dance to loud country music playing on the juke box. One couple looked like they were practically holding each other up, while the other was slow-dancing in circles, barely avoiding stepping on each others' feet.

"You hungry, honey?" Judy asked. She handed Mary a Coke and a bag of potato chips. "This ain't much, but it'll get you through tonight. Sorry all of this is happening."

Mary was grateful to be with her parents, even if it was in the bar. She wondered if the stranger had called again after she left the house. She imagined the phone ringing endlessly and an exasperated pervert scowling in disappointment when no one answered. Feeling antsy, Mary tapped her mother on the arm. Judy leaned over to hear her whisper, "Can I go play the games?"

Judy thought for a moment and looked for Robert before answering. "Yeah, but don't be walking around here otherwise," she warned. "Your daddy says you can sit here, play the games, or go to the bathroom. That's it, okay? Oh, and don't play the poker machine. Somehow that don't seem right, a little girl playing poker."

Mary walked over to the games with a handful of quarters from the tip jar. She decided to play the one with the spaceships first. She was glad when she realized that the smoke wasn't as thick around that area.

After playing for a few minutes, Mary felt pressure on her back. She realized that someone was leaning into her. Glancing over her shoulder, she saw Devin looking down at her with a smile. The feel of him so close was warm and exciting. She panicked and quickly looked back at the game.

"Whoa, girl, you're about to lose your spaceship," he said, as he reached around her and put his hand on hers to play the game. His body pressed against her a little harder. She was keenly aware of the heat passing between them.

Mary didn't know how to react to what was happening. The rush of emotions was overwhelming. Here was this guy –– this grown man –– that she'd had a crush on ever since she could remember. And he was standing close to her and touching her hand. It felt like electricity was racing through her entire body as she struggled to stand still. She wanted to turn around and face him, but she had no idea what to do or how to do it. Instead, she let him guide her hand on the joystick.

"I'm sure glad your daddy brought you back here tonight," he said, focusing on the screen of the game.

Awkwardly, Mary searched for the words to answer him, but couldn't think of any.

"So, there was some guy bugging you on the phone?" he asked.

"Yes," Mary managed to answer.

"That's not right, you know?"

"I was scared."

"I know you were. But I would never let anything happen to you."

Mary looked up to see Devin gazing directly into her eyes with what Mary could only assume was pure passion. She felt hot and embarrassed. "Your mama told me you thought I was handsome one time," he said. "Do you still think that? Because I think you're beautiful." He wasn't smiling. He was dead serious.

Had the world gone crazy? A feeling that Mary couldn't define washed over her. It almost felt like guilt. Was it guilt? She didn't know why she felt that way. She had done nothing wrong.

Mary was conscious of the fact that her parents were keeping an eye on her, so she tried to snap out of this trance of desire that had a hold of her. If her daddy saw her like this, what would he think? She opened her mouth to respond to Devin, but was interrupted by her mother who happened to be walking past.

"Hey, you two. What's going on over here?" Judy said as she winked at Devin, obviously unaware of the intensity of their conversation. "Try not to beat Devin too much on these games, you hear?" she said to Mary with a smile as she walked away with her hands full of empty beer cups.

Mary was stunned that her mother couldn't see what was going on since her body seemed to be screaming out that she wanted this man to embrace her. It was like a siren, loud and clear, and bigger than anything Mary had ever felt in her whole life. How could anyone not see it?

"Uh, I need to go to the bathroom," she said suddenly, as she pushed her way out of Devin's hold. He took a step back to give her room to get past him. When she looked up at him, his eyes were staring right into hers.

Passing the dance floor, Mary noticed that only one couple was still dancing. They were looking at each other intensely, smiling. Mary thought she knew what they were feeling and looked away out of new-found respect. After all, she now knew what passion and desire felt like.

Once in the bathroom, Mary looked at herself in the mirror and thought about the events of the night. First, some weirdo calls her and scares her out of her mind, and now a man she really liked was acting like he wanted her in a grown-up way. She wondered if she was starting to look like a woman. *Is age twelve the turning point when men start noticing you?* she wondered. And is this what it's like to have a boyfriend? She felt like she had crossed some kind of threshold into womanhood. It felt good, but scary and forbidden. She'd have to keep her relationship with Devin secret. She'd tell Melanie, of course, but no one else.

Mary stood up straight and looked at herself in the mirror sideways. *He must think I'm pretty.* Trying to reflect on what she must have looked like when Devin was talking to her, she smiled and fluttered her eyes in the mirror. *I should've worn makeup tonight. Look at all those goofy freckles.* "I don't know if I'm ready for all of this," she sighed, as she walked out of the bathroom.

Mary was surprised to find that Devin was nowhere in sight when she exited the restroom. By now, closing time was fast approaching and the number of people in the bar was thinning out. Judy was wiping the empty tables down with a rag. A few stragglers were finishing their beers and saying their drunken goodbyes.

Had Devin left without even saying anything to her? She watched to see if maybe he had just gone to the bathroom. A couple of men came and went from it, but no Devin. She felt a pang of regret and a little bit of relief.

A woman was putting on lipstick at one of the tables, peering into a small hand-held mirror. She was an older woman, and she looked all wrinkly. Mary wondered why the lady even bothered — the night was pretty much over, and no men were around to even give her a second look. Besides, it was dark in the bar, and what difference would a little lipstick mean anyway? *A waste of time*, Mary thought. When the woman saw Mary watching her, she acted embarrassed, grabbed her purse, and left.

After realizing that Devin really was gone, Mary felt let down and wanted to go home. A sense of emptiness filled her, and she found no comfort in her usual overactive imagination. She couldn't even pretend not to feel bad about his come-on and the let-down that followed. She figured he must be a very insensitive man to act that way.

The last customer in the bar was asleep, leaned back against the wall in his chair. Mary felt like walking over and kicking it out from underneath him. Judy tapped the man on the shoulder and told him it was closing time. He grunted, picked his hat up off the floor, and staggered to the door. Just outside the bar, he dropped his keys and cussed when he couldn't find them in the darkness.

Chapter 7

"Oh, Melanie, I'm in love!" Mary gushed as she hugged her friend tight. "And he loves me, too!"

Melanie pulled away and looked at her for a moment. "Mary, you're just a kid to him. He's grown up and you're just twelve years old. He does not love you."

It felt like Melanie had thrown a whole cup of acid in her face. "Are you kidding me?" she demanded. "You didn't see his eyes and hear what he said. Yes, he does love me."

Mel rolled her eyes. "He was probably drunk. And why were you there in the first place? You're not supposed to be going there. My mama said so."

Mary was hurt that her friend didn't share her enthusiasm for the situation. She surmised that Melanie was just too young to understand. After all, she was a year younger than Mary. *No wonder she doesn't get it*, Mary thought. "Well, whatever. It's starting to get late. I guess I'm going home now."

"All right, Sugar!" Melanie made kissy faces to her as she waved goodbye.

"Oh, shut up," Mary said sullenly.

The sunset was beautiful to Mary as she walked down the hill and back to her house. As stunning as it was, though, it didn't lift her spirits, and it couldn't undo the words that Melanie had said. *Maybe she's right. Maybe Devin doesn't like me, but I sure hope he does.*

When Mary got home, the house was full of people. The radio was on, and couples were slow-dancing in the living room. It was Sunday night, and since the bar wasn't open, the party had ended up at their house.

Mary grabbed something from the kitchen to eat in her room. The last thing she wanted was to be around a bunch of drunk people. Heading down the hallway, she noticed her father asleep on his bed. She wondered where her mother was. *If it wasn't dark already, I swear I'd go to the barn.*

After eating, Mary closed her eyes and started thinking about Devin and what had happened at the bar the night before. She imagined him lying in bed with her, feeling his breath on her neck, his hands on her body. She felt like she had memorized every word he had said.

Had he really abandoned her at the bar? No, he wouldn't have done that. He must have been sick and needed to go home. Maybe he just couldn't take that place anymore. Mary understood that feeling and imagined that he was actually a sensitive man with no tolerance for ignorance. She once again turned her memories back to the sound of his voice. It was sweet and familiar, and she missed the sound of it so much she ached in her chest. Never having known the feeling of a yearning heart, she wondered if maybe she too was getting sick.

Mary drifted off to sleep and awoke to someone yelling from somewhere in the house. Sitting straight up, she realized it was dark outside and probably pretty late. There was no clock in the room, and she felt the need to know what time it was for some reason.

She opened the door to find her mother in the hallway yelling at her father. "Robert get up now, come on, we've got to go help him!"

"What?" Robert yelled.

"Right now, come on!"

Mary's father was attempting to sit up in the bed, but he was so drunk his eyes looked like they were pasted shut. "I am up, dammit, I am!" he said, slurring his words.

Judy stomped into the bedroom and pulled at his arms. When she let go of them, they flopped back down onto the bed. She put her hands on her hips and glared at him.

"What's going on?" Mary asked as she walked down the hallway past her parents' bedroom. No one answered. She heard people moving around in the living room, so she went to see what was happening.

Someone grabbed her by the shoulders and turned her around. "Mary, somebody's holding a knife on your brother at the laundromat," the man told her. The last word came out as "laundry-mat". He stood up straight, revealing his unimpressive height. He wasn't much taller than Mary herself.

"Huh? What brother?" Mary asked, confused and disoriented. *Who are these people anyway?*

"Just come on. Let's go get in the car," the man said. He looked rough with a lot of facial hair and tattoos on his arms and neck. Mary was disgusted by the acne pits in his face. She assumed that was why he had a full mustache and beard.

"But where's my mama and daddy?"

"They're coming. Look, you don't even have any shoes on. Come on, girl, we've got to go."

Mary spotted her flip-flops under the edge of a chair and quickly put them on. She looked back and saw her father stumbling into the living room. He kept leaning against the wall for support.

"Robert, come on!" Judy pleaded.

"Honey, I can't drive. I can't even see. I need to lay back down." His voice trailed off, and he looked for a place to sit down or fall down.

"Oh, no you don't," she said, as she dragged him by the arm toward the door. She glanced over at the fireplace, and at the last minute before heading outside, she ran back and grabbed the poker. Robert watched her and yawned. As she pushed him out the door, Mary could hear him fussing.

Mary got into the car with the man with the acne pits and a woman she recognized as being another friend of her parents'. She could tell they were both drunk, and they seemed very agitated about something, though they didn't say much. The woman kept turning around in her seat to look out the back window of the car.

"What's happening?" Mary asked.

"Didn't anybody tell you? It's your brother. He's in trouble."

Mary counted six cars driving away from her house, including the one she was riding in. There were at least two people in each one. Their shadows in the dim light of passing cars seemed evil, heads together, plotting and scheming.

Within a few minutes, they arrived at a neighborhood of small, older houses, all right next to each other. Mary knew the area; it was right in the middle of town. She went to school with a lot of kids who lived there and passed it every day on the school bus.

The caravan of cars led by Mary's parents wound through the neighborhood like a drunken parade. Finally, they all pulled into the driveway and onto the street in front of a little white house. The neighborhood was quiet except for slamming doors as everyone got out of their vehicles. The man who was driving the car Mary had ridden in picked her up and sat her on the hood of the car. "You stay here. Don't go anywhere, okay?"

Mary nodded. She saw her parents go up to the front door of the house. Her Daddy appeared to have sobered up some -- probably because of the intensity of the moment, Mary reasoned. She watched her mother raise the fireplace poker and rap on the door with it. The sound of it echoed and dogs started barking nearby.

The porch light came on as the door opened slightly. Mary couldn't see who had opened it, but she saw her parents push their way inside. Her parents' friends started closing in on the house as well. They converged on the place like a swarm of bees, most of them entering the front door. A couple of guys stayed on the front porch and watched like spectators at some bizarre sporting event. One went around the back of the house.

A fat girl ran out of the house yelling, "Call the police!" panting hard as she passed Mary. She ran down the road out of sight. Frowning, Mary focused her attention back to the scene at the house. *I can't help anybody right now.*

Everything looked like it was moving in slow motion. Screams and shouts came from the house, and it appeared to be literally shaking. One guy seemed confused as to what to do, so he kicked a dog in the yard. The poor dog yelped, and the man went into the house, which was already bursting at the seams with people.

Minutes later, everyone ran out of the house in a hurry. A couple of people tried to run out the door at the same time, clumsily getting stuck as they struggled to get out. Mary thought it was funny and laughed out loud. She quickly cast aside any humor she'd found in the situation as soon as she saw her parents.

Robert and Judy were the last to exit. Mary was shocked to see that her Daddy had blood all over his face. She slid off the hood of the car and ran toward her parents, crying as she looked at her father. "Daddy, you got shot in the face!" she yelled. Sobbing, she contemplated throwing her arms around him. But she was scared to touch him, and clung to her mother instead.

"Get in," Robert said as he shoved Mary into the car. "Judy, calm her down."

"Your daddy wasn't shot, honey," Judy said. "He's fine."

"The hell I am." Robert was holding a handkerchief to his forehead. Blood was all over his shirt and hands.

Mary was terrified and couldn't stop crying. "Can't you please tell me what's going on?" Mary begged her mother.

Judy was visibly shaken. She put her arm around Mary and answered, "Your daddy got hit in the face with the fireplace poker."

Once they got back to Robert and Judy's house, everyone filtered in and settled in the living room. It was like they were all on some type of high as they began to recount what they had done.

Robert had cleaned his face up and changed shirts. Someone had put a bandage on his forehead, and it was already soaked through with blood. He slumped on the couch and opened a beer.

"You all right?" Judy asked, her face wrinkled with concern.

"Yeah, I'm all right. I guess I'm fine." He took a deep breath and sat back. "It's my own fault. I shouldn't have thrown the poker at them bitches. They just picked it up and wham! Hit me right in the face with it. But not before I cracked their heads together." He demonstrated with his hands what he was describing.

Everyone in the room laughed. One guy was doubled over and giggled, "I didn't know what the hell to do, so I kicked the damn dog!" He stopped laughing abruptly and declared, "Don't worry. I picked the poker up off the floor and threw it in my back seat. After we left, I slung the motherfucker off into a field as far as I could send it. Ain't nobody gonna find it now, I guarantee."

Mary felt dizzy as she looked around the room at the drunken, macabre characters. She whispered to her mother, "Please, Mama, make them go home now. I want them all to leave, okay?" Anxiety overwhelmed her.

"Shh!" Judy gave her daughter a look of warning to be quiet.

"What do you think is going on over there now?" Robert asked nobody in particular, gingerly touching his sore forehead.

"I don't know. Let's go find out," answered the man with the acne pits that Mary had ridden with earlier. She wondered what his name was. He sure looked mean.

So everyone got into their cars again and drove back to the scene of the crime to see what was going on. It seemed inconceivable to Mary that this was happening. *Why are we doing this? Are they really that stupid?* At that moment, all she wanted was to be safe at home with all these crazy people long gone.

This time Mary rode with her parents. She kept quiet and stared at the illuminated numbers on the dashboard of the car. *No wonder people don't like my family. Look at how they act.* She wondered what Devin would think of the situation. She was sure he wouldn't approve.

When they got back to the little white house, there was an ambulance on the scene. Mary's parents started laughing hysterically. "Like somebody over there is really hurt!" Judy said mockingly, cackling like she was insane.

"Those assholes'll think twice before messing with us again, huh?"

Once everyone circled the neighborhood and got back on the main road headed back to Robert and Judy's house, they honked their horns, and some even stuck their arms out the windows, shaking their fists in the air. *This is beyond ridiculous. These people are a bunch of small-time hooligans,* Mary thought. *They're actually proud of what they've done. But what are they getting out of this? What're they trying to prove? None of it makes any sense.*

She sat back in her seat, fidgeting, aching to be at home in her own bed, dreaming about something good. Her head hurt from crying, but she knew it didn't hurt as much as her daddy's. She hoped he would wear the bandage for a good while. She wasn't ready to look at the hole in his forehead again anytime soon.

Mary figured the police would be waiting for them when they arrived home. She was sure they'd take her parents away and she'd never see them again. Isn't that what happens in situations like this? She started crying softly to herself again. Her whole world seemed to be crumbling around her.

Chapter 8

"You've been served," the policeman said as he handed Robert a handful of papers at the front door. With a worried look on his face, Robert turned to say something to Judy, only to find that she was standing right behind him.

"What's that?" she pointed to the papers in his hand.

"Well, uh, I guess we have to go to court for what we did."

Judy sat down on the couch and looked at the papers. "Attempted murder, assault and battery. . . Now what are we supposed to do?"

"I guess we need to get a lawyer."

"We don't have any money for a lawyer," Judy moaned, as she sat back on the couch and looked at the ceiling.

"Well, you might have thought about that before you drug me out of bed, drunker than a boiled owl, and made me drive you to those peoples' house to beat the shit out of them with a fireplace poker!" Robert yelled in her face.

"You knew I couldn't drive when you married me!" Judy screamed back.

"Yeah, but I didn't think you'd be asking me to drive you to commit attempted murder on a bunch of scumbags that ain't worth killing!"

"No, you're the one who went in there and started beating everybody up. I just took that poker to show that I meant business. I wasn't going to use it on anybody!"

"Yeah, right. You're always itching for a fight, ain't you? Well, you got one now! You get the lawyer; it's all your damn fault!" Robert slammed the door behind him as he left the house, rattling the windows.

"Where's he going?" Mary asked.

"He's got to open up the bar. He'll probably be drunk by the time I get over there," Judy answered as she hung her head and started to cry.

Mary tried to think of something positive to say. Finally she said, "I guess it could be worse. The police could have come and arrested everybody that night."

Judy stopped crying and looked at her daughter. "You know what? I'm surprised they didn't. And maybe it would've been a good thing if they had."

Mary sighed. "Why do y'all have to be fighting all the time? I mean, why can't we just be like normal people?"

Mary saw a flash of contempt in her mother's eyes. Judy opened her mouth like she was going to yell at her daughter, but apparently caught herself, as she seemed to deliberately choose her words. "What's normal? Huh? I ain't seen normal yet in my life. You kids think you have it so rough, you don't know nothing." Her tone bitter, she paused to get Mary's reaction. She continued, "Your daddy only married me so I'd have you. I didn't want another baby. I was done."

Mary recoiled at her mother's hateful words. "Another baby?" was all she managed to say.

"Yeah, another damned baby!" Judy said through clenched teeth.

The look on her mother's face was too much to bear. Mary ran out the door and toward the barn. The baby pigs were grunting and sticking their little snouts through the fence as Mary squatted to pet them. "You dumb pigs are lucky," she said as she looked into their innocent eyes. "You don't even know how bad things can be."

Mary dejectedly wiped away her tears and looked at the sun setting in the distance. She threw a scoop of corn into the pig trough. The hungry little pigs gobbled it up, rooting each other out of the way to look for any kernels that might have escaped them.

Mary decided she needed to get away and be by herself for a while. With no particular destination in mind, she left the barn, and walked up the driveway. Looking back, she wished her mother would come out onto the porch and ask her to stay home. The house looked deserted, and Mary felt empty. Somewhere she heard dogs barking and wondered where Chester was. She realized she hadn't seen him in days.

The evening had turned out to be hazy, and the air seemed stagnant to Mary. She considered going to Melanie's house, but she felt too down to see anyone, even her best friend. She just needed to get some things straight in her head. Her heart felt like it weighed a ton as she trudged along, thinking about what might happen with her family.

The thought occurred to her that her parents might go to jail. She almost liked that idea. Maybe she would get to live with Melanie. She smiled as she daydreamed about it, imagining sleeping in the same bed with her friend every night, telling ghost stories and giggling about silly things.

A white truck with a blue top passed her and slowed down. Mary glanced at it and kept walking. There wasn't a lot of traffic on this back road, and she paid attention to it out of habit. She didn't recognize the truck, but then she realized she really didn't know everybody who lived along the road.

A few minutes later, she heard a vehicle behind her and looked back to see headlights that she realized, upon studying further, were attached to the same white and blue truck. She couldn't make out who was inside, but she could tell it was a man. He passed her slowly and revved the engine as he got down the road a bit.

Mary wondered if she should turn back and go home. She decided that was probably a good idea. She turned around and began walking quickly back toward her house. Her heart was hammering in her chest as she looked behind her to see if the truck was in sight. It wasn't, and she breathed a sigh of relief, still picking up her pace to get home as quickly as possible.

As Mary walked past Melanie's house, she heard the truck again, coming up behind her. It slowed down until it had practically stopped. She felt like this was becoming a bad situation, so she took off running through the field next to Melanie's house.

She realized that she was approaching a cemetery. Tripping over some rocks piled up at the entrance, she grabbed onto a sign to steady herself. It said "Hill

Cemetary". Mary noticed that the word "cemetery" was misspelled and made a mental note to tell someone about that later.

Looking for a place to hide, she saw a tombstone shaped like a harp. It was taller than the others and wide as well. She quickly ran behind it and crouched as much as she could, hoping that it hid her. Her hand was bleeding, and she looked down to see a splinter in her finger. *I'll get that out later*, she thought to herself.

Mary strained to see the road, squinting in the darkness. The gravestones were black silhouettes against the darkening sky, and she couldn't tell if the truck had parked or driven away. Straining to hear, she leaned her head forward against the tombstone to balance her weight.

She could tell that the wind had picked up, and she heard crickets. Their chirping sounded like it was coming in waves. She then heard the crispy sound of footsteps on dry grass. It was slight, and she wasn't sure if she was really just hearing her own feet as she changed positions. She listened harder, trying to block out the sound of the crickets. There it was again, the sound of footsteps, and this time she knew she hadn't moved.

There was a whistling sound. *Is somebody whistling?* Mary wondered. She speculated whether it was the wind or a person. Her heart was pounding now, and she felt sick to her stomach. She closed her eyes and prayed, *God, please let me be okay.*

Mary's feet gave way from underneath her as she precariously shifted to get a better look out into the graveyard. She saw movement. It looked like a man, and he was walking right toward her, the footsteps steady and heavy. Mary fell back onto the ground, but quickly regained the strength to pull herself up onto her feet.

"Leave me alone!" she screamed as she looked at the figure coming toward her. He didn't stop, and she was terrified. "Leave me alone!" she screamed again as she searched for somewhere else to hide. Behind the cemetery she saw the black outline of a barn.

Running toward the barn, she instinctively slowed down, wondering if there would be a fence between the graveyard and the barn. Her eyes scanned the landscape to see if she needed to get ready to crawl under or climb over one. She was relieved when she realized there was no fence with which she'd have to contend.

Mary brushed away a spider web that clung to her hair like a sticky net as she ran into the entrance of the barn. Though darkness was closing in, Mary could see that there were tobacco stalks lying around the floor of the barn.

The barn smelled of a wet mustiness that was usually a comfort to Mary; however, she found no consolation in it at that moment. Right now it was heavily oppressive, invading her senses, heightening her awareness of her isolation.

Mary was scared to look behind her to see where her pursuer was. She needed a place to hide, so she ran inside one of the stalls, then scooted behind the rickety door and listened. She heard nothing.

Who is this that's chasing me? she wondered. *Is it Devin?* No, Devin loved her; he wouldn't do something like this. She knew it wasn't Doc. The truck certainly didn't belong to him; he didn't drive -- he walked everywhere. *Is it the man on the phone who called and said dirty words to me?* Maybe. What about the beady-eyed guy who was drinking with her parents and had followed her to the pigpen? The sneering faces of her parents' friends went around and around in Mary's mind. She remembered their voices and the words they used. *Nobody even knows where I am,* she realized. *Somebody's going to get me, and nobody will even know who it was.*

The door Mary was hiding behind began to push against her. The pressure of it was almost suffocating as she stifled a scream. She felt the need to turn sideways so that it didn't crush her face. A bright light was coming toward her, faint at first then ultra-bright, making her turn away from it. *Is that a flashlight?* She thought. *God, that's the brightest light I've ever seen. It's hot; I need to get out of here.* Mary pushed against the pressure of the door but finally gave up. It was too much. She rested her head against the stall door, closed her eyes, and surrendered to an unknown force.

Chapter 9

"Mary," a voice said, sounding thick.

"Huh?" Mary answered. She was vaguely aware of someone touching her hand.

"Mary, are you all right?"

"I don't understand what you're saying. Give me a minute. My mouth is dry; I need some water." Mary's own voice sounded foreign to her.

"I think you're still too sleepy to talk right now," she heard a woman say.

"No, no, I'm awake. Where am I?" The room smelled like disinfectant and rubbing alcohol.

"You're at the hospital, honey. You're okay, though. We're going to help you."

Mary felt sick. She opened her eyes and focused on the bright light above her. "I don't feel good."

"I'm sure you don't. Just lay still for a few minutes. Don't try to sit up just yet. You've been asleep for a while."

"Where are my parents? Do they know I'm here?" Mary asked, her voice tinged with desperation. She glanced up to see a woman dressed in a white hospital coat looking at her sympathetically.

"No, they're not here."

"But where are they?"

"Let's talk about this later, okay?"

"No, I want to know where they are!"

Hesitating for a moment, the doctor seemed to be looking for the right words to say. Finally she answered, "Mary, your parents passed away a long time ago."

"Oh, no. That's not true. I was just with them. I have to go find them," Mary struggled to get up, and realized that her arms were strapped down. "I don't understand this. Please help me!"

The doctor pushed a button on the side of the bed, and she attempted to pat Mary's shoulder. Mary looked at her wildly and strained to free herself. "What the heck is this? I want to go home."

Two large men dressed in scrubs walked in and stood on opposite sides of her bed, preparing to hold her down while the doctor pulled a needle out of her pocket and popped the cap off.

"No, no, I don't need that. I'll be good. I'll lay still, please, don't do that!"

The doctor paused and looked at her. "You're going to calm down so we can talk? I don't want you hurting yourself."

"I will. I promise." Mary went limp, feeling exhausted.

The orderlies left the room, and the doctor sat in a chair next to Mary's bed. "Mary, my name is Dr. Powell. Presently, you're under my care. You've had a rough patch, and you were admitted to this psychiatric ward about two weeks ago. You probably don't remember anything about being admitted, as you were in a really bad way when you arrived. Your sister brought you in."

Mary stared at the doctor. "What sister?"

"Your older sister – the one you live with," answered the doctor.

There was no response from Mary. She stared blankly at the doctor.

"You've had a manic episode. I had to administer sedatives so you could get some rest. . . I believe that has clouded your memory somewhat." The doctor paused and continued. "I know you're confused right now. You do have a sister, and you also had a brother."

"Really? I do? Are you kidding me?"

The doctor answered, "Yes, you do, and no, I'm not. Technically, they're your half brother and sister. You all have the same mother. Don't you remember growing up around them?"

"Growing up? But I'm just a kid. I'm only twelve." Mary looked at the doctor like she had lost her mind.

Dr. Powell studied Mary's face for a moment, then answered softly, "Mary, dear, you're thirty-five years old."

The room seemed to be closing in on Mary. How could this be happening? She didn't even know who she was anymore. "My parents are dead?"

"Yes, I'm afraid they died in an accident years ago. You have been in and out of hospitals since then. Do you remember talking to doctors before?"

"Yes. I mean, not really. Not like this. And not with you."

"That's right, you and I have never met."

"So, what now? How long am I going to be here?"

"I'm not exactly sure yet. Your sister has been taking good care of you, but I want to keep you here for a while for evaluation. I think soon you will be on your way to a better place, mentally, but I want to take a good, overall look at your physical health before taking your treatment to the next level. As a resident of the ward, I believe you will benefit highly from the therapy you will receive here. I'll make your well-being my mission." She smiled and patted Mary's hand.

Mary wanted to slap the doctor for her patronizing attitude, but she decided it would be a better idea to play along. "Can I please have my hands free? I won't do anything crazy. I just need to be able to move a little."

The doctor nodded and smiled. "Yes, I think the worst of this episode is over." She leaned over Mary and unfastened the straps around her wrists. "There, is that better? I'm going to have them bring you something to eat. Don't rush it. I don't want you getting sick. We will talk later this afternoon after you've had time to rest. Feel free to get up and go to the bathroom as needed. If you need anything, push this button," she said. "Oh, and we can see you at all times, so just know that we're keeping you safe."

Mary looked around the room and saw a reflective window that she assumed was the vantage point from which the staff watched her. She couldn't actually see anything in it except for a reflection of her own room. She felt resentful about being watched, but she didn't say anything, or else the doctor might restrain her again. She smiled and nodded at the doctor, keeping her complaints to herself.

After eating the bland food that was brought to her, Mary decided to look around the room. She saw a bathroom with a shower in it. She decided that it would feel good to clean up. She wondered how long it had been since she'd had a bath.

As she pulled off her hospital gown, she looked around to determine if anyone could see her. The reflective window was not in her view, so she assumed she at least had bathroom privacy. Surely she deserved that much consideration.

Looking in the mirror, she was surprised to see her own reflection. It took a few seconds to realize she really was a grown lady! She even saw a few grey hairs at her temples and little lines around her eyes.

This can't be real, she thought, touching her face. She looked down at her obviously adult body. She stared at herself in the mirror in amazement.

I'm not grown, I know I'm not! She started to cry softly. *Oh, God, I look like my mother when I cry*, she sobbed, holding onto a bar bolted into the wall for support. "I need my mother!" she screamed. "Mama! Oh, God, somebody please get my mama for me!"

Mary stumbled to the bed, overcome with grief. She pushed the button for help, but the doctor and an orderly were already coming through the door. They looked ominous to her, with serious looks on their faces. *This can't be good*, she thought to herself. *These people look really mean!*

"Now Mary, I thought we were going to calm down. Dear, I don't want to sedate you, but we have to get a handle on this," the doctor said as she attempted to get Mary to sit down.

"I hate this place. Please, just let me go home!" Mary screamed as she pushed the doctor away. "Ow!" she yelled as she felt a pinch on her arm. She looked down to see the doctor injecting something into her, but she didn't have the strength to fight it.

"I hate you assholes!" Mary shouted, the room spinning around her. She fell sideways into the bed and didn't have the strength to roll over onto her back. She tasted and smelled medicine, and everything faded away.

Chapter 10

Mary walked up the hill to her friend Melanie's house. *The air smells so fresh after all that rain,* she thought as she breathed deeply and looked at the pretty, blue sky. The clouds were still heavy-looking, with darkness on the horizon, but the sun shone brilliantly through them. As she reached Melanie's house, she saw several cars she didn't recognize -- fancy cars that had license plates from another state.

Melanie met Mary in the yard. "Let's go for a walk somewhere," she said, rolling her eyes.

"What's going on, do you have company?" Mary asked, looking back at Melanie's house.

"Not company, exactly. It's my uncle and his family. Oh, and there are a bunch of Arabs up there," she said in a whisper, even though no one could hear her talking.

"Arabs?"

"I have no idea why, but there are a bunch of them up there, and my uncle is using our house to host them."

"Are they actually staying there? Sleeping there?"

"No, but this is the second day they've come here, and I really wish they'd go somewhere else. They just wander around like they don't have anything to do. It's weird!"

"Wow. Well, you have to show them to me before I go home. I've never seen anything like that."

Mary and Melanie walked through a field to look at the horses that were fenced in a nearby pasture. "Those horses are so beautiful," Mary said, as she sat on a stump near the fence.

"Yeah," Melanie sighed.

Mary could tell something was bothering her friend. She was sure it was because she had strangers in her house. "Why is your uncle meeting with those people at your house? Why doesn't he just meet with them at his own house?"

"I'm not sure. I don't know why he'd come all the way here to meet up with a bunch of people from another country. I asked my mother, but she just shook her head and didn't really give me an answer. I don't think she knows either."

The girls started walking, neither of them saying anything. Mary was about to ask a question when Melanie said with a sneaky smile, "Let's go back to my house. You really have to see this."

Mary laughed at her friend. She was so dramatic sometimes. They took turns kicking a hedge-apple down the dirt road back to Melanie's house.

As the girls walked up to the house, they saw a man with a turban standing in the yard with his arms crossed. He seemed uninterested in them, with a bored look on his face. There was no acknowledgement toward him from Melanie either as she walked past him. Mary had to stop herself from staring at the man, and noted that he had on regular clothes — a pair of slacks and a shirt neatly tucked in, buttoned all the way to his neck. He had a fancy-looking watch at which he kept looking.

Once inside, Mary noticed cigarette smoke. "I didn't know your mama allowed people to smoke in the house."

"She doesn't. But it's like this hasn't even been our house for the past few days. She tells me that they're all supposed to leave by the end of the weekend."

The girls got a drink from the kitchen and sat on the couch. Mary looked at all the people standing around. She looked at Melanie and stifled a giggle. "That man over there. . . his maroon turban matches his maroon pants," she whispered.

"I know!" Melanie said, looking away from Mary. "Quit looking at me, you're gonna make me laugh."

A different man, dressed in a full Arab outfit, walked into the living room from the hallway that led to the bedrooms. He focused on Mary sitting on the couch, and he approached her. Mary panicked and looked at the floor. This was beyond funny. He reached out and took her hand, which was resting on her thigh, pulled it toward him, and kissed it gently. "You are a beautiful young lady." His eyes were intense, and he did not waver from staring right into her face. She forced herself to look back at him.

In the most serious tone she could manage, Mary answered, "Thank you."

Melanie had her hand over her mouth, trying not to laugh.

As the man released Mary's hand, he nodded to her, ceremoniously straightened up, and walked back down the hallway and toward the back of the house.

Mary sat with her mouth ajar, wondering what had just happened. She looked at her friend, who had a mocking look on her face. "Stop making fun of me," Mary said defensively. "How am I supposed to know how to act when something like that happens?"

"Let's go back outside. It's too crowded in here," Melanie said as she pulled Mary by the arm toward the door. "I feel like they're listening to me when I talk."

When they were halfway down the hill, Mary asked, "What are these jokers doing here in the middle of nowhere, out here in the country where there are just a bunch of cows and chickens? I don't get it."

"I've been trying to figure that out myself. Everything's all hush-hush. My uncle just calls them 'business associates'. I don't know what that means. Stay for dinner, okay? It'll be hilarious, watching these guys."

"Ooh, did you see that guy kiss my hand? I didn't know if he was gonna try to bite me or what," Mary joked. Melanie laughed until she got the hiccups. Then Mary laughed at Melanie's hiccups. She was spent by the time they got down the hill.

As evening approached, the girls went back to the house so they wouldn't miss the show of foreigners at the dinner table. They sat across from each other at the table so they could gauge each other's reaction to the scene about to unfold.

While Melanie's mother was placing the food on the table, various people started filtering into the dining room. The man with the maroon turban sat down first and smiled at the girls. A woman and a man sat down next. Mary recognized the man as Melanie's uncle, who she had met once before, and she assumed the woman was his wife.

A man who was sitting in the living room with his back to everyone stood up and came into the dining room. He looked important with his suit and tie. He nodded to everyone as he stood behind the chair in which he was about to sit. Melanie's uncle nodded back to him, and Mary deduced that this was a man of importance. Maybe he was the guest of honor. He sat next to her, and she tried desperately not to stare at him.

"Please pass the potatoes," he said to Mary as he smiled warmly at her. He had a thick accent which she didn't recognize.

"Yeah, don't just sit there, start passing the food around," Melanie's uncle said. "You'll have to forgive us, we're from the country!" He laughed as if he was kidding, but Mary could hear the aggravation in his voice.

"Sorry. Here you go," she said, her hands shaking under the weight of the heavy bowl of mashed potatoes.

"Thank you," he said kindly. "My name is Henry."

"Henry is the President of Honduras," Melanie's uncle said abruptly. His wife nudged him with her elbow and opened her eyes wide as if to tell him to shut up. The prideful look on his face quickly turned sour.

"That's quite all right. Really. I'm happy to meet everyone here," Henry said in his thick accent.

Mary stared at Melanie, who looked stunned at this revelation. Her eyebrows went up and she shrugged. For the rest of the meal, Mary was quiet, speaking only when spoken to. She sensed the significance of the moment and focused on not embarrassing herself. She was afraid she'd spill or get strangled on her water, so she didn't drink anything throughout dinner. She choked down her food, wishing the fiasco was over so she could talk to her friend.

Stealing glances at Melanie, she tried not to look at her for very long, for fear that either or both of them would start giggling. She didn't want to get in trouble in front of all these people. Sure enough, though, a lingering glance made Melanie stifle a laugh. *These people are going to think we're so silly and juvenile.*

"Where are you girls going?" asked Melanie's mother, as she cleared the table after dinner.

"Just up to my room," Melanie answered, practically pushing Mary down the hallway.

"Okay. What was that all about?" Mary asked, once they were safe in Melanie's room. "Was that really the President of Honduras?"

"I don't know. That's the first I've heard of it."

"He spoke English. What language do they speak in Honduras, anyway?"

Melanie shrugged. "Did you see my mama look at my uncle like this?" Melanie frowned and pursed her lips together.

"I did see that. I think she was trying to tell him to shut up. Wow, you have some crazy things going on at your house," Mary said, shaking her head in disbelief. "I love it. It's like a movie or something."

"Well, I can't wait till they leave. I just want those weirdoes to get out of my house."

Mary sat on the edge of Melanie's bed and briefly looked through a magazine she had laying on the nightstand. She looked at the clock and realized it was getting late. "I hate to say it, but I'm going to have to go home. Got to go to school tomorrow."

"You know, I never really told you, but I hate it when you go home. I can't stand that you have to go back there."

"Y'all could adopt me," Mary joked, but Melanie didn't respond. Mary looked at her friend, who seemed genuinely sad at the thought of her leaving. She put her arm around Melanie's shoulders. "Oh, Mel, I'll be all right. You'll be all right, too. Looks like your mama wants those people to leave as bad as you do. See you on the bus tomorrow."

Chapter 11

"Did you hear the news?" Melanie said to Mary in a hushed voice.

"What news?" Mary said, as she settled in next to her friend on the porch swing.

"Remember those foreigners that were at my house a few weeks ago?"

"Oh, yeah, how could I forget?" Mary said, grinning.

"Well, you won't believe this, but my uncle has been arrested!"

"Are you kidding me? Why?"

"Get this -- he was selling guns and stuff to those people with turbans, and to that man who said he was the President of Honduras!"

Mary sat slack-jawed. "Selling guns? How many guns does he have?"

"No, silly, not selling them his own guns. Selling them guns and bombs from somebody else. He was kind of like a middleman, or so my mama says. I think he was making money by helping someone else sell weapons to those people."

"Are you serious? That sounds so dangerous! Were there guns and bombs in your house?" Mary asked, mesmerized by the whole conversation. It sounded like something out of a spy novel.

Melanie laughed at the look on Mary's face. "No, no. I don't know where they were. I don't know any details. I just know that he was doing illegal stuff in our house! Now my mama is afraid they'll take our house away from us."

"Oh. Well, that probably won't happen."

"I don't know. She's scared living in that house now. She's talking about us moving back to town."

Mary thought about what her friend said and felt sick at the thought of Melanie not living next door anymore. She wished she had something to say that would turn the conversation around, but nothing came to her. She hugged Melanie and said she needed to go home.

Why did Mel's uncle have to come here and get everybody involved in the bad stuff he was doing? Mary wondered as she walked back to her house, dragging her feet along the gravel driveway. She couldn't imagine being alone again without anyone to talk to, and no one could replace her friend.

Later that evening, Mary lay in bed replaying the conversations she'd had with Melanie. The fact that there might have been an international weapons operation going on in the house right next door didn't scare her nearly as much as the thought of her friend moving away. She buried her face in her pillow and cried. *Please, God, don't take Melanie away from me.*

The week went by fast for Mary, as she moped around feeling sorry for herself. She didn't ask Melanie anything about moving, hoping that if she just didn't bring it up it wouldn't happen. The thought never left her mind, though.

Saturday morning, Mary woke up to a cat lying on top of her. "Get off me, silly!" she said, gently moving the cat onto the bed. As she got dressed, she heard her mother yelling outside and looked out the window to see Judy running out of the outhouse, clumsily pulling up her pants. Mary went to see what was happening.

"Good Lord, I think there's a snake in there! Lord help me!" shrieked Judy, rubbing her backside with her hand.

"What in the world?" Robert said as he threw down his hammer on the concrete patio beside the well house. He ran toward Judy, his spare tire bouncing with every step.

Judy looked enraged as she turned to Robert, pointing in his face. "You better get that damned pump fixed or whatever it is you have to do, because I am tired of using that friggin' outhouse! If I didn't have to shit like a crippled coon, I wouldn't have even used it!" Tears ran down her cheeks as she jabbed her finger into Robert's chest. "I'm sick of wasps and spiders, and there are probably even snakes in there, and something just bit me on my ass! This is the 1980s, dammit! I want running water and an indoor bathroom that I can use!"

Robert looked surprised and disappointed at the same time. He didn't answer; he just walked back toward the well house shaking his head. Judy watched him walk away, her chest heaving with anger.

By then, Mary was petting Chester in the driveway, and pretended not to be troubled by the fight between her parents. But she felt a deep sense of sadness and longed for something that she couldn't define. She stood up to go for a walk; the destination seemed unimportant.

Mary slapped the dirt off her knees as she headed up the driveway. Chester started to follow, but Mary hollered at him to stay. Looking dejected, he reluctantly sat down and watched her leave.

Glancing back, Mary didn't see her father at the well house any more, and she didn't see her mother either. She picked up a stick off the ground and kept walking. "I hate this place," she whispered to herself as she threw the stick as far as she could into a ditch.

She walked down to the creek and sat down on a big rock that jutted out from the bank. She watched a bunch of tadpoles swimming in a little pool of water created by rocks, which almost looked like they had been placed intentionally for that purpose.

The rushing sound of the creek made her feel like she had to pee, so she looked for a bush to hide behind, pulled down her pants and squatted. As she was about to stand up, she heard a man's voice. He was mumbling, and it sounded like he was out of breath. On his shoulder, he was carrying something. He was struggling with the weight of it and walked cautiously to balance it out. Mary looked hard at him and what he was carrying. It was a person!

Mary crouched back down behind the bush and peered through the leaves. She realized she was holding her breath as she listened. Her pants were still down at her ankles. She thought about how impossible it would be to run if it came down to it.

The man was young-looking, wearing a baseball cap that was perched precariously on his head, threatening to fall off with every step. With his free hand, he pulled it back down securely onto his head.

As the man got near the water, he fought to keep his footing on the loose rocks of the creek bank. He carefully stepped onto a mossy area that made a squishing sound. Once he secured a position where his feet seemed steady, he leaned forward and dumped the body on the ground. It landed with a small splash as the head of the person hit the water.

Mary gasped as she realized it was her mother. She stared in horror at her mother's grey skin, her limp body. Mary's legs were weak. She started feeling tingly all over, and she was afraid she was going to faint. Ripples of fear fluttered through her body as she watched her mother's hair floating in the water at the edge of the creek.

In the process of dropping the body on the ground, the man's hat fell off into the water. "Shit!" he hissed as he picked it up, knocked the excess water off against his jeans, then put it back on his head and left.

Mary swallowed hard to keep from getting sick. She was afraid he would come back to get her, too, but she had to go help her mother. As soon as she was fairly sure the man was gone, she quickly pulled up her pants, which she couldn't remember how to fasten in her nervous haste to get to her mother's body.

She approached her mother slowly, as if she might really be alive and all of this was just a morbid joke –

maybe it was a surprise, kind of like a jack-in-the-box --- her mother sitting straight up to say "Gotcha!"

She cautiously put her hands to her mother's drawn, leathery face and noticed that she had a rope tied tight around her neck. *Who would do this?*

Mary backed up and sat on the big rock for a moment, unable to comprehend what she was seeing. Suddenly aware of sound again, she heard a woodpecker somewhere in the woods pecking its little head off. She didn't know what to do next, so she got up and ran through the field toward her house. Her feet felt heavy, as if she were running in mud. *Daddy will need me when he finds out what's happened. But what do we do? He'll know what to do.*

"Daddy!" Mary screamed, out of breath from running. "Daddy, where are you?" She stopped to listen. No response. The pigs were oinking and squealing, but the rest of the place was fairly quiet.

Mary ran toward the barn, the safest place she knew. As she ran past the outhouse, she could see the pigs playing in their pen with something. They yanked at it, played tug-of-war with it. Mary slowed her running down and almost tripped over her own feet when she realized that the pigs were chewing on a shirt. It was the blue flannel shirt her father wore all the time.

Walking toward the pig pen, Mary concentrated on breathing. She was out of breath from running. Every time she inhaled, her lungs burned. She approached the baby pigs, which could hardly be called babies any more since they'd gotten so big, and watched them do whatever they were doing. *What are they doing?* She leaned forward and looked hard at them.

At first, it seemed like maybe one of the pigs had gotten caught under the trough, and the other pigs were ravaging it, feeding on their own cannibalistic frenzy. But then Mary saw a muddy hand sticking out from under the trough that the pigs were tugging at. She realized it must be her father's body trapped under the trough. *Who else could it be?* The pigs were trying to pull him out from under it, bumping into each other as they worked to get a good hold on him.

"Shoo! Stop that!" Mary screamed. Looking around for something to distract the pigs, she threw the biggest rock she could find at them. It didn't hit any of them, instead landing in the mud with a thick, splattering thud. They looked unfazed as they continued gnawing on her father's hand and wrist, oinking at each other, and fighting for a turn at his flesh.

One of the pigs, its snout covered with blood, stopped momentarily to look at Mary with indifference. The sounds of their chewing, and their feet making sucking sounds in the mud as they repositioned themselves for better access to his body was sickening. They sniffed and snorted; it sounded like they were enjoying themselves thoroughly.

Paralyzed for a moment, Mary briefly considered getting into the pigpen to save her father. All she could see were his arms and legs sticking out from under the trough, his torso completely blocked from her view. *He's dead; I know it,* she thought. *And those are not the same baby pigs I played with. They're mean! They'll eat me, too!*

Mary started running toward the house, calling for her dog. "Chester!" she shouted as loud as she could. But her voice was weak, and it sounded like a whisper to her. When she got to the well house, she noticed that the cover was off. With a heavy feeling, she approached it. A sense of foreboding gripped her, causing her to shake; but she knew she had to look inside. So she climbed the ladder and cautiously peered into the well house. She saw her father's head lying on the plywood floor next to the pump; the eyes were open and bloodshot. Mary stared at her father's wild looking face. *Oh my God, somebody cut Daddy's head off, flung it over into this well house, and chucked his body into the pig pen!*

Straightening herself up, Mary looked up at the sky. A scream that came out of somewhere in her body that she didn't know existed finally escaped as she wobbled on the ladder, trying not to fall. As the ladder slipped under her weight, she struggled to grab onto the side of the well house. The wood was rough, and the skin on her hands felt raw as she held on with all her strength. The pain intense, she let go and fell backwards onto the ground, her head banging against the concrete patio.

Chapter 12

Mary snuggled underneath a blanket, feeling warm and rested. She smelled food. It smelled like something good, maybe pizza. She realized she hadn't eaten in a long time.

"Mary, it's Dr. Powell."

Mary opened her eyes and saw the doctor, smiling down at her.

"I'm so hungry."

"That's a good sign."

"I'm scared, though, because I've been having some awful dreams," Mary said weakly.

"I know. I've been watching you. You haven't been still for a minute."

"Can I have something to eat?"

"You sure can." Dr. Powell turned to the intercom on the side of the bed. "Please bring Mary a tray. She's ready to eat now."

She turned back to Mary. "I'm going to send a nurse in here to help you get cleaned up and get you ready to put some food in that tummy of yours," Dr. Powell said to Mary as if she was a slow-thinking dummy. Mary felt slightly offended by it. "You and I are going to have a talk after you've eaten and get an idea of how you feel about things. Don't you worry; you're going to be okay." She closed the door as she left the room.

When the food came, Mary ate half of her soup and a piece of bread. She felt better, though a headache seemed to be lingering. She wondered how long she'd been asleep.

"Can I get something for this headache?" she asked into the intercom next to the bed. She noticed that her fingernails were long, and she made a mental note to ask for some clippers later.

"One moment, please," a woman's voice answered.

Dr. Powell walked in with two pills in a little white cup. "Here, take these."

Mary swallowed the pills, washing them down with what was left of the weak tea they'd given her, and looked at the doctor. "Okay, I'm ready to talk now."

"Oh?"

"Yes, ma'am. I kind of need your help to figure some things out."

Dr. Powell smiled and pulled up a chair next to Mary's bed. "Mary, I am so glad to hear you say that. How do you feel today?"

"Besides this headache, I actually feel pretty good. I really wish I could go home. This place stinks. No offense."

"None taken."

"Really, I don't want to stay here. When can I leave?"

"We'll get to that, I promise. Did you get enough to eat?"

"Yeah, but it didn't taste very good."

Dr. Powell laughed, "Yes, I'm sure that's true."

"I really want to get out of here. This place is not good for me. What do I need to do?"

"Maybe we can start out by talking about why you're here. Does that sound okay to you?"

"Yes."

"First of all, let's talk about your self-image. We touched on this, but then you sort of freaked out about it and we haven't discussed it since then. You do realize that you are a grown-up lady, right?"

"I know you told me I am, and when I see myself, it looks like it."

"But do you believe that it's true?"

"Yes, of course. I do believe it's true. I just don't know how I got here — to this stage of my life, that is. I only remember being a girl. I don't even remember graduating high school. Where did I go to school?"

"You didn't get all the way through high school, I'm afraid. You've been in and out of hospitals over the years, and it seems as though you have blocked out a big part of your life from your memory."

Mary stared at the woman, trying to tell if she was lying to her.

"Mary, your parents died when you were a little girl. I think you were about twelve when that happened. Do you remember your parents passing away?"

"Yes, and it was awful!" Mary cried and put her hands over her face. She hoped the doctor wasn't going to torture her with rehashing what had happened. Why go through all of that? What good would it do?

"You're right, it was. They died in a car accident. You were with them, and thankfully, you survived. Do you remember when that happened?"

"Wait a minute, how can that be true?" she said through tears that had made her eyes sore already. "They were murdered. I know it! I saw their bodies!"

Dr. Powell placed her hand on Mary's. "No, that's not what happened, Mary. You are confusing a dream with reality. Honey, I have a copy of their death certificates in your file, and I have also talked to your sister."

Mary looked away from the doctor and stared out the window. Dr. Powell patiently waited a moment before continuing, "Think about it. Tell me what you remember about your family. Anything you can remember is good; one memory almost always leads to another."

Mary's mind reeled. She was afraid the doctor was really going to think she was crazy if she couldn't even remember her own brother and sister. She was keenly aware of Dr. Powell watching her and taking notes. She didn't want to give her any more ammunition to keep her in this godforsaken hospital.

Images of people she had known in her life came to mind. She shuffled through them, trying to recognize who they might be. Everything seemed to be jumbled together as she tried to focus on figuring it out. She could feel the doctor scrutinizing her, and the minutes seemed like hours as she scrambled for an answer to give the doctor. Why was this so hard? Why couldn't she just come up with the memory of these people and the things that had happened to them?

Finally, she accepted the fact that she had a sister. It seemed plausible enough. Somewhere in the back of her mind, she remembered a woman who was kind to her. No, it wasn't her mother, but it was a woman who looked like her. *Yes, that has to be my sister,* Mary concluded. But a brother? She could not figure out who that person was. *Maybe the doctor made it up. Now, why would she do that?*

"Yes, you told me I had a brother and a sister. I'm sure I remember a sister, but where's my brother?" Mary asked, narrowing her eyes suspiciously at her doctor. She picked at her cuticles anxiously, oblivious to the fact that she was already drawing blood on one of her fingers.

Dr. Powell stood up and walked toward the window. She turned around to face Mary with an encouraging look on her face. "I was hoping you could tell me." She handed Mary a tissue. Mary looked at her questioningly. "For your finger."

"Oh. Thank you," Mary said as she dabbed at the blood that had formed in a little bubble at the base of her fingernail. She looked at the doctor expectantly.

Dr. Powell sighed and looked back at Mary. "So, what can you tell me?"

"Huh?" Mary looked skeptically at the doctor. "If I knew, would I be asking you?" Mary knew her voice sounded edgy, but she didn't care. This charade was getting out of hand. It felt like the doctor was playing a guessing game, and she was getting weary of it.

"It sounds like we're spinning our wheels on this subject today. I don't want to upset you. Perhaps we can talk about this some more at our next session. You're closer than you think to coming up with your own answers."

"Why can't you just tell me?"

"Mary, I want you to answer your own questions," Dr. Powell repeated. "I know that sounds backwards, but I really want you to remember things on your own. Don't worry, I'm going to help you."

"Well, can't you help me now? How about giving me an idea as to what happened to my brother? Why is it that I can't even picture this person? You know, don't you? I think you should just tell me what happened. Where's this supposed brother of mine?" Mary was indignant, waiting for a response.

"I'm afraid that's where the story gets a little muddy," Dr. Powell said. "Again, I think that we should have that conversation on another day. For now, you rest."

Chapter 13

Devin smiled with approval as Mary scooted up next to him at the bar. She was stunned by his good looks as she stared at his reflection in the mirror behind the bar.

Mary leaned toward Devin and whispered, "I'm not even supposed to be here, but Mama and Daddy couldn't find anybody to watch me tonight." *There I go again!* She immediately realized that she must sound like a big baby. *Mama and Daddy couldn't find anybody to watch me? Silly me!*

"Well, I'm glad you're here." Devin casually draped his arm around Mary's shoulders. Evidently, what she said hadn't fazed him. He was sitting so close to her she could smell him; he smelled like detergent, very clean. Mary wondered if he did his own laundry or if he had a girlfriend. She smiled at him and hoped she was at least as pretty as any girlfriend he might have.

"Thanks," Mary said, searching for words.

"So, did that nasty man ever call you again?"

"You mean the one that was saying bad things to me on the phone?" Mary felt like biting her tongue. Of course that's who he meant!

"Yeah, that bad old man who was talking dirty to you," Devin smiled seductively, and it made Mary's stomach turn flips. Mary liked the look of the dark stubble on his chin. She wanted to reach out and touch it. His eyes were so brown, she wanted to stare into them forever.

"No, he didn't, but. . ." Before Mary could finish her sentence, a man walked up and sat down on a bar stool on the other side of Devin.

"How you doin', buddy?" he asked Devin.

"Aw, hey, how's it going?" Devin answered, patting him on the back.

"You trying to hit on my sister or something?"

"Naw, Dee! She's just a cute little girl." He turned his back to Mary as he talked to her brother.

Mary felt embarrassed and out of place. She couldn't believe the rudeness of her brother, interrupting her conversation with the man that she loved. She sat and listened to the men talking, trying to figure out a graceful way of walking away. They were laughing and acting like old friends, making her feel like an outsider.

"Give me a call sometime. Let's go hunting or something," Dee said, lifting his baseball cap to scratch his head. "We have some woods behind the house, and there's plenty of deer back there with your name on 'em!" He then turned to Mary as he got up to walk away. "Now, you don't bother my buddy here too much, okay? He don't want to be sitting here wasting his time talking to a little kid." His tone was admonishing. Mary shrank in his gaze.

Devin lit a cigarette and faced forward. Mary didn't know what to say, so she looked at her hands. She felt foolish and wanted to run away.

"I guess your brother watches out for you all the time, huh?" Devin asked, still staring straight ahead. His profile was beautiful.

Mary detected a slight tone of disappointment in his voice. At this point, she knew it was hopeless. The damage had been done. "I hate him. He sticks his nose in my business all the time." She knew she sounded like a pouting baby, but at this point, who cared?

Devin glanced at her and took a drag of his cigarette. "Looks to me like he's just looking out for you. I don't want him after me for talking to you, that's for sure. He'd kick my ass in a New York minute."

"He doesn't run my life, and he doesn't know how we feel about each other," Mary said a bit too defensively. She immediately wished she knew when to shut up when she looked at Devin. The expression on his face surprised her. He was frowning and smiling at the same time, shaking his head slowly.

"I don't feel anything for you, Mary, except friendship. If you think I ever did, then you just misunderstood, that's all." His voice was flat and emotionless. Fiddling with a bottle top that was laying on the bar, he seemed to be detached from the conversation. He put his cigarette butt in the little bit of beer that was left in his bottle and threw a dollar on the bar. Without even looking back at Mary, he got down from his stool and walked toward the door to leave.

The rejection stung like a hundred bees all over her body. *Please let him turn around and tell me goodbye or something. Please don't let him just leave!* Mary thought desperately, her throat tightening with resentment toward her brother and sadness for the man she loved as he walked away.

She thought about following him outside. *He'll talk to me there, and no one will interrupt us. I know he has some things he wants to tell me.* For a few seconds, she weighed his reaction against her longing to hear him say he really loved her. The fear of hearing the opposite stopped her in her tracks.

As Devin walked out the door, Mary felt her disappointment turn into bitter hatred toward her brother. She looked around for her parents and noticed that her father was already pretty drunk, laughing loudly with a woman at the end of the bar. Her mother was nowhere in sight.

Mary saw her brother leaning against the juke box, helping some trampy-looking girl pick out a song. It made Mary want to puke, watching him make his moves on her. The girl smiled at him and put her hand on his chest. *Bastard.*

Mary went to look for her mother. It was almost closing time, and the few people left in the bar were making their way out the door. She found her mother behind the bar, doing a final cleanup. "Closing time!" Judy called out, before she realized everyone had already left.

"You about ready to go?" Judy said to Mary as she closed the refrigerated beer cooler. "Where's Dee?"

"I have no idea, and I don't care," Mary answered flippantly.

"I think he's going to have to get a ride home with us. He's pretty wasted."

"And Daddy's in better shape to drive?" Mary asked with raised eyebrows, feeling aggravated that her mother refused to drive.

"Well, I sure can't drive! Don't worry, your daddy is fine," Judy answered dismissively.

When they got to the car, Mary shot a nasty look at her brother. "I'm not riding in the backseat with him."

"Shit," Dee said as he fell into the backseat. His baseball cap fell into the floor as he attempted to straighten himself up in the seat.

"You ride up front with your daddy, and I'll ride back here with Dee," Judy said, obviously annoyed at her kids' rivalry.

Robert sat staring straight ahead, waiting for the argument to end. "Somebody close his door," he said motioning toward Dee in the backseat. When nobody moved, Robert threw open his door, got out and slammed the back door.

Mary sulked in the front seat. She fought back tears as she replayed the vision of Devin walking out of the bar, not even speaking to her before he left. She crossed her arms and watched the car lights go by.

"I feel sick." Dee seemed wide awake all of a sudden.

"Robert, pull over, he's sick," Judy said, tapping on Robert's shoulder.

Mary covered her ears as her brother got sick out of his open car door. When he closed the door, Robert glanced back at him, "You all right now?"

Dee nodded. "Yeah."

Robert got back on the road. Mary noticed that he cautiously watched the rear view mirror for traffic. *I guess Mama's right,* she thought. *Maybe he is sober enough to get us home.* Her brother moaned from the backseat.

"Mama, make him be quiet," Mary said. The sound of his voice made her angry.

"Shut up, bimbo," Dee grumbled.

Mary turned around to see him frowning at her. "No, you shut up, asshole!"

"Hey, we're not going to talk to each other that way! You pop-eyed younguns gotta be fighting all the time?" Judy said angrily, yanking a handful of Mary's hair.

"Ow! Why did you do that? He started it!"

"I don't care who started it!" Judy answered.

"You always take his side of everything!"

"And you always keep some shit stirred up!" Dee said, leaning forward in his seat to get in her face.

Mary reached back to smack him, but he moved, making her slap the back of her father's head instead. "Goddammit, stop it!" yelled Robert as he looked angrily at Mary.

"Why is it always me?" Mary screamed louder than she meant to.

"Robert, pull over this car. I'm going to whip her ass," Judy said.

"No, don't!" Mary pleaded as her father started to pull over to the side of the road. She reached for the steering wheel.

"Let go right now, Mary!" Robert yelled as he pushed her off of him.

Mary turned loose of the steering wheel. As Robert tried to get control of the car, he turned the wheel too far, and it began to veer off to the side. A bridge over a train track was immediately in front of them now, and it seemed as if the car was pulling itself toward it.

"Hey, Robert?" Judy yelled from the back seat.

Mary watched her father instinctively throw his arm in front of her as he lost control of the car. It went over the side of the bridge. Mary braced herself as she saw the railroad tracks rocketing toward her.

Chapter 14

"What do you think about this one?" Mary asked, holding up a dress.

"Try it on and let's see."

Mary pulled the dress over her head and zipped it up on the side. She posed, awaiting her friend's opinion.

Melanie looked at her disapprovingly. "I think it makes you look too skinny," Melanie answered thoughtfully. "Yes, it definitely does."

Mary looked at her friend disgustedly. "Well, excuse me!" She knew she was being defensive about it, but she hated being skinny. Worse than that, she hated when other people called her skinny.

Laughing, Melanie put her hands on Mary's shoulders and said, "You're not going to a beauty contest. Nobody cares what you look like."

"Yeah, I know." Mary sat on the bed and played with the hem of her dress nervously.

Melanie sat next to Mary, rifling through her purse looking for something. She finally pulled a brush out of it and proceeded to clean all the hair out of the bristles. Mary was momentarily captivated by Melanie's preoccupation with removing hair from her brush. She wished she could just sit there all day with her friend, doing meaningless stuff like that; Melanie's life seemed so much easier than hers. The jealousy she felt was a heavy burden at times because she loved Melanie so much.

Mary said abruptly, "Ain't this something — my parents having to go to court over that crazy thing they did, breaking into that house and beating up those people?"

"That was just plain weird," Melanie answered, running the newly-cleaned brush through her hair.

"I've never been in a court room before. I wonder what it's like."

"Oh, just some wrinkled-up old judge sitting behind a stand. 'Hear ye, hear ye. All rise! We are here to put these crazy people in jail for acting like dumbasses'," Melanie announced, pretending like she was holding a gavel, pounding the brush against her open hand.

Mary laughed. "You go in my place and tell me how it went!" She was only half-kidding.

"Uh, I don't think so. Just go and pretend you're watching TV or something."

"Sure, that's what I'll do. And then I'll turn the channel when Daddy gets up on the stand and shows everybody the poker scar on his forehead," Mary said sarcastically.

Melanie giggled and said, "You know, you really never told me why your parents did that. And weren't you scared when you went with them that night?"

Mary thought for a minute before she spoke. She sat on the edge of the bed and studied her shoes. *Dang, these are ugly shoes.* Finally she said, "Mel, all I know is that somebody drew a knife on my brother at the laundromat. I don't know what that family had to do with what went on, exactly, except I think they were already in a feud, and they probably just wanted something to fight about. They're like that, you know, my parents. They love to fight with each other, other people, us kids. They thrive on it."

"Did someone cut your brother?"

"No, I don't think so. He's fine as far as I know. I don't think they did anything bad to him, actually."

"What are you going to do if your parents really do have to go to jail?"

Mary considered what Melanie said. "I don't know. I never seriously thought about that. What if they do?"

"You can come live with me." Melanie smiled at her, with tears in her eyes.

"And I would, too, believe me," Mary cried, and hugged her friend. She was touched that Mel was so open with her emotions. She didn't want to let go of her; she wanted the moment to never end. She sniffed and wiped her nose on her sleeve, then realized she'd just demonstrated the worst manners ever and blushed.

Melanie smiled. "Okay. Off you go. Call me when you get back home."

Mary walked down the hill to her house. She looked back to see Melanie wave at her and motion for her to call later. Mary nodded back.

Chester ran up to Mary and attempted to put his paws on her. "No, don't do that!" she said quickly. "You might get me dirty." She bent down to pet her sweet dog. He looked at her and whined.

"Oh, Chester, you're the only good thing about this place, you know that? You stink, and you have a bunch of ticks on you all the time, but you're still better than the rest of us."

The dog rolled over onto his back and pleaded with his eyes to be rubbed. His incessant whining was shrill and insistent. Mary all of a sudden felt sorry for him. After all, it wasn't his fault he wasn't clean and shiny and tick-free like Melanie's dogs. After some contemplation, though, she concluded that he was an outside dog, and outside dogs are very different from inside dogs. The clarification seemed reasonable, and Mary dismissed any thoughts of pity for him.

"No, I'm not going to scratch your belly right now. I have to go. Why don't you go play with the kitty cats, huh?" She petted the top of his nose, which seemed to be the cleanest spot on his body, then stepped around him and went into her house.

Mary heard her parents getting ready for court as she walked in the front door. "I'm home!" she yelled as she walked toward the bathroom.

"Home from where?" Judy asked, sticking her head out of the bedroom to answer. She had on a housecoat and slippers. She always got dressed last thing before heading out the door so she wouldn't get make-up on her clothes. Mary smiled a little at the sight of it. *At least some things stay the same*, she thought. "Never mind," she answered, with a heavy sigh.

She heard her mother ask her father why he couldn't be more careful with his shaving. Their voices were like a dozen fingernails on a dozen chalkboards, as incessant and shrill as Chester's whining sometimes.

Mary leaned on the doorjamb to the bathroom, observing the predictable bickering between her parents. "I'm just nervous, that's all," Robert said as he stuck little pieces of toilet tissue to the bleeding razor cuts on his chin. He stood a few inches from the mirror, scanning his chin and neck for any remaining nicks that might need bits of tissue stuck to them.

"What'd you do, shave with a hatchet?" Judy joked.

"Ha ha. You are so funny," Robert answered dryly.

"Well, if you go in there with your face all cut up like that, they're going to think you're some kind of rough character," Judy pointed out.

"Yeah, yeah. I know." By then Robert was using a styptic pencil to stop the bleeding.

"Mary, go see if your brother is ready," Judy said as she sprayed a cloud of hairspray around her head. She had teased her hair up as usual.

Walking down the hallway, Mary already knew what kind of response she'd get from Dee. She stuck her head in the doorway of his bedroom. "You almost ready?"

He flipped the bird at her, and Mary yelled to her mother, "Yeah, he's ready!"

"You're going to jail today, jackass!" Mary hissed at her brother before turning to leave. She heard him say "bullshit" as she walked down the hallway.

"Now listen, we're going to deny, deny, deny when we get into that courtroom today. Don't volunteer anything, and don't say anything about each other, either. You hear?" Robert lectured as everyone got into the car.

Robert's shirt was wrinkled, and he still had blood on his face from shaving. Mary turned away, disgusted with the sight of him, yet ashamed of her own embarrassment. He had a hangover, and he smelled like body odor. All she wanted was for the day to be over.

"You remember your own advice," Judy said with a smirk.

"Well, you just remember who ran back into the house to grab the poker!" Robert snapped, his words dripping with contempt.

"What poker?"

Robert smiled. "Exactly."

Chapter 15

The courtroom was smaller than Mary had imagined. It smelled old, and it looked generic and outdated. She had anticipated it would be a little statelier, with padded seats and fancy curtains. Instead, there were hard, wooden pew-like benches, yellowed blinds on the windows, and the floors were covered with cheap-looking, well-worn linoleum.

Somehow Mary had thought it would just be her family and the people they had attacked, but the courtroom was full of other people there for various reasons. As cases were called, people approached podiums, facing the judge. Mary was surprised at how quickly the judge moved people through the process. Few people had attorneys representing them; she guessed that they were all probably as poor as her parents and couldn't afford one.

An occasional cough interrupted the court proceedings, and there were whispers throughout the room. Mary just knew they were all talking about her family. She tried to be as inconspicuous as possible, inching away from her parents to the edge of the bench.

Finally, a man in a uniform announced that her parents' case was next. *At least that part is like what I've seen on TV.*

Robert and Judy made their way to a podium, and opposite of them at the other podium were three women who Mary assumed were the people her parents had attacked. They were all heavy-set women with short hair, cut kind of like a man's. One of them had on a neck brace, and they all looked miserable.

Mary stared at the three ladies, wondering why her parents would have assaulted them and what they had to do with her brother. They certainly looked rough, and Mary avoided staring at them for very long for fear they would figure out who she was and give her a mean look.

The judge bent his head down and looked over his glasses at Robert, Judy, and Dee. He seemed to be studying them as his assistant handed him the file on the case.

"What do we have here?" he asked as he looked through the file. "Does either side have an attorney present today?" No one answered, so the judge continued, "I guess that means no. So, who got hit by. . .

wait a minute, does this say a fireplace poker?" The judge looked at his assistant, who shrugged.

"I did, Your Honor. And that man right over there hit me with it!" answered the woman with the neck brace smugly as she pointed her chubby finger at Robert. She was apparently the spokesperson for the group of women and took her role as such very seriously.

Mary noticed that one of the other women's stomach was so fat it hung like an apron around her waist, and she had a double-chin that shook when she moved. Her black, cropped-off hair revealed a tattoo on the side of her neck that Mary couldn't make out. It looked like it was probably meant to be a butterfly, but the fat folds of her neck distorted it, making it look like a big, colorful blob.

"Is that true?" the judge asked Robert.

"No sir, that's not true. I never hit that woman with anything."

The judge looked at Robert for a moment, paused, and turned back to the large woman with the neck brace. "Tell me your side of the story, ma'am."

"Well, sir, that young man over there was dating my daughter." She pointed to Dee, who looked bored and stared at the floor. "He got her pregnant and refused to take responsibility for it."

The judge looked at Dee. He looked back at the judge and shook his head.

"Go on, ma'am," said the judge.

"So, my son went to find him and talk some sense into him. He ain't gonna take somebody mistreating his sister. Well, anyway, he saw him driving down the road and they both pulled over to talk at the laundromat. That's all I know. Then the next thing I know, those people were banging on my door, and they came into the house and beat up on me, my daughter who's pregnant, and my sister." The woman was clearly agitated and scowled as she talked. The words came out of her mouth with such ferocity that she practically spit them out.

The judge had a look of aggravated impatience on his face, but he remained silent and listened. He fiddled with something on his desk, and appeared to be forcing himself to pay attention to what was being said. He acknowledged the woman's statement: "Uh huh."

Her eyes narrowed as she looked at Robert. "And that man right here, that man, he hit me with a poker and punched me and my daughter right in the face."

"And why didn't you just go ahead and have them arrested that night?" The judge raised his eyebrows, as if he was expecting a bogus answer.

"Well, I, uh. . . I was in shock."

"In shock, or had something to hide? Maybe you didn't want the police in your house that night."

The word "police" came out as "po-leece", and Mary smiled.

"Ma'am, do you take street drugs? Smoke marijuana?" the judge asked. His jowls hung low, kind of like Chester's, which made him look funny and serious at the same time.

The woman looked at him in disbelief for a moment before stammering, "Uh, no, of course not."

The woman's indignant tone made the judge smile disdainfully. "Hmm, of course not." He took a deep breath and leaned forward, addressing Robert. "Sir, what is your side of this?"

Robert answered, "Your Honor, yes, we did go to their house to talk to them that night. We heard that a bunch of no-good guys were holding a knife to our son's throat because her daughter set it up as some kind of revenge thing. We went to the laundromat first, but no one was there." He held up his hand to the sky and continued, "I pray you believe me when I say we never hurt anybody in that house."

Mary wanted to laugh at her father's dramatic plea to the judge. She was amazed at the lies coming out of his mouth. She felt stunned, too, listening to the words he spoke, wondering if he was going to go to jail, Hell or both for his disregard of his oath on the Bible. It seemed to come so natural for him, and Mary was almost impressed with his ability to come across so believably.

The judge seemed unimpressed as he looked at Robert. Apparently her daddy's story wasn't as believable to him as it was to Mary. Before the judge could respond, the large spokeswoman from the plaintiff's side started shouting. Startled, the judge looked at her, surprised by her outburst.

"He's lying! He did so come into our home and try to kill us. My daughter got a hold of that poker and she hit him right square between his eyes! Just look at his face. You can probably see where she hit him!" yelled the woman, her face screwed up and flushed with anger. The sight of her sticking her bottom lip out was almost too much.

"Shh!" The woman with the fat apron bumped her and mouthed the words *shut up*. The spokeswoman realized she was probably saying too much, and nodded to the other woman that she'd be quiet. The third woman had said nothing the entire time. She stood behind the other two women, as if she were trying to avoid the situation entirely. Mary figured that she must be the girl Dee had gotten pregnant. That he would have done such a thing didn't surprise her at all. It was just like Dee to get a girl pregnant and dump her.

The judge sat silent for a moment before continuing. Visibly exasperated with the plaintiffs, he turned his attention to Dee. "Son, did somebody cut you at the Wishy Wash?" he said mockingly.

To Mary's surprise, people in the courtroom laughed. It seemed as though the judge wasn't even taking this case seriously. She didn't know if that was a good sign or not.

"No, sir."

"Make that 'No, Your Honor' when you're talking to a judge, boy!" the judge growled with anger. He apparently wanted to make an example of Dee's bad manners as he looked around the courtroom for a reaction. He didn't get one.

Dee nodded his acknowledgement of the judge's reprimand. The judge raised his eyebrows to which he responded, "Yes, sir, Your Honor."

"Does anybody have any medical bills, pictures, or evidence in this case?" said the judge.

The three women looked at each other. "I have whiplash from them people beating on me, and it's a wonder my daughter didn't have a miscarriage!" said the woman who had been doing all the talking.

"Where is the alleged poker?" asked the judge dryly, not even bothering to hide his disgust for the pathetic scene before him.

Robert shrugged and the women shook their heads, eyeing Robert and Judy suspiciously. Mary of course knew that the poker was laying out in a field somewhere, thrown by that goofy guy who bragged about getting rid of the evidence that night. She almost felt guilty herself just for knowing the truth.

"I'm going to have to dismiss this case due to lack of evidence unless somebody can show me right now why we should continue."

"Can't you tell them people to leave us alone and never bother us again?" whined the woman with the neck brace.

"Ma'am, you will have to get a restraining order if you want them to stay away from you." He looked at Robert, "And yes, you need to stay away from these women and their house." He pointed his gavel at Dee, "And son, if you really are the father of this girl's baby over here, be a man and do the right thing."

Dee nodded to the judge and looked away. As he turned away from the judge, Mary saw him smile arrogantly, as if he had gotten away with something.

Chapter 16

Mary's sister Darlene was sitting in a chair in the corner when Mary walked into the doctor's office for her therapy session. Darlene stood up to hug her, but Mary's unreceptive, stiff posture made it clear that she didn't want to be hugged.

"How are you doing?" Darlene asked as she backed away and took her seat.

"I'm fine," Mary answered with no emotion. "I feel just fine." She forced a smile. Turning to the doctor, Mary asked, "What's she doing here?"

"I thought it was time we talked about the progress of your therapy, and I figured you would probably like to visit with your sister. You do recognize her as your sister, don't you, Mary?"

"Of course I do," Mary answered, acting insulted. "Why wouldn't I know my own family?"

After several seconds of silence, Darlene changed the subject. "I, um, brought you some of your favorite books. I thought you might like to catch up on some of your reading."

There was no reply from Mary. She sat looking at the floor.

"I can bring you anything else you need from home. All you need to do is let me know. Okay?"

"Okay. Thanks." Mary continued to stare at the floor. She shifted in her seat, turning slightly away from her sister.

"So, do you feel like you're getting back to normal, Mary? I mean, I'm really looking forward to taking you home when you're ready. But the doctor has to say you're ready, and you have to tell me yourself how you feel about it." Darlene seemed to be searching for words to say, and they sounded forced.

Mary looked up at Darlene, her face blank. "Did you just ask me if I feel back to normal? I don't even know what normal is!" Mary suddenly remembered her mother saying that once.

Darlene's face turned red, like she was embarrassed in front of the doctor.

"Now, why would she ask me something like that?" Mary looked at the doctor for support.

Dr. Powell didn't answer. She watched the sisters' interaction without intervening. She showed no intention of mediating their conversation. Writing notes in Mary's file, she occasionally looked up at them.

"I didn't mean that you should just be ready to walk out of here today or anything," Darlene said defensively. "I only meant that I want to know how you feel and see what the doctor has to say. That's all. Don't get all mad at me for trying to do what's right for you."

Mary reflected on what her sister had said, and softened her tone. "I'm sorry. I just don't know how to handle all of this. Sometimes I don't even know what's real and what isn't."

"All I've ever done is try to help you." Darlene picked at imaginary lint on her pants to avoid looking at Mary.

"Yes, I know that. I appreciate it." Mary felt like crying, but she took a deep breath and stopped herself from giving in to it. "Oh, by the way, I had a dream that Doc died."

"Really? Aw, that's too bad." Darlene looked at the doctor questioningly, as if she wasn't sure what to say.

"Yeah, I dreamed he saw a rattlesnake and it shook him up so bad he went home and had a heart attack."

"Well, I'll be." Darlene had a fake look of surprise plastered on her face.

"He was a funny old guy." Mary's words hung out in the air like a Wednesday washing on a clothesline. Heavy and tiresome.

There was a pause in the conversation that seemed infinite. Mary felt the need to fill the silence. She turned to the doctor. "Did I tell you about Doc? One time he came to the house, and Mama was in the yard. This was a few years after we moved out there to that shitty house in the country, and Doc came walking down the driveway. And since it was the first time we'd ever met him, we didn't know he couldn't talk plain."

Darlene smiled patronizingly.

"Well, anyway, so here comes Doc down the driveway, and he walks up to Mama and says, 'Yownt tum tootumbies?'"

With an amused look on her face, Darlene listened patiently. She almost looked as if she were waiting for the punch line of a joke.

Dr. Powell took more notes. Mary wondered what she was writing. *And why doesn't Darlene think this is funny? This is so funny!*

"So Mama looks at me. And I look at her. And we have no idea what he's talking about. He says it again, 'Yownt tum tootumbies?'" Mary made a face like Doc for effect. "And then he reaches down into a paper bag he's carrying and pulls out a cucumber!"

With a chuckle, Darlene asked, "So tootumbies are cucumbers?"

Laughing, Mary said, "Yes, and then he asked her if she wanted a 'bushel of tweet taties' and a 'passel of maties'."

Obviously placating Mary, Darlene answered, "I guess that meant sweet potatoes or tomatoes, right?"

"Yeah, that's right!" Mary, momentarily oblivious to the fact she was in a therapy session, laughed uproariously. Suddenly aware of Dr. Powell's presence, she looked at her nervously, afraid she was breaking some kind of rule by having this kind of frivolous conversation. What if the doctor is analyzing her behavior and finds her to be a stupid idiot with no sense of how to act? *She thinks I'm a fruitcake, I'm sure of it.* She composed herself and concocted what she thought to be a normal, pleasant expression.

Dr. Powell was smiling as she winked at Darlene. The doctor then looked back at Mary. "No worries. It's okay; I'm glad to see you having a good time. I'm also happy to hear you talk about things you remember from your past."

Darlene looked confused. She appeared to be waiting for someone else to say something.

Mary cleared her throat and looked back down at the floor. She knew she had strayed off course too much. More than that, she felt silly — like she had brought up something that nobody remembered, and now she looked like a fool.

Dr. Powell stood up and walked around her desk to face Mary and her sister. She leaned against a chair and crossed her arms. Mary studied the doctor perhaps for the first time since she'd been there. From the time she'd arrived, the doctor seemed like a fixture to her. A person who just happened to belong at the hospital. Not human, not pretty, not ugly. Just a necessary, soon-to-be forgotten instrument to gauge her own sanity. Surely she didn't have real emotions or even a life outside this hospital. But looking at Dr. Powell at that moment, and *really* studying her, Mary realized that she probably had a husband, maybe a family, laughed and cried like everybody else. With short black hair, big blue eyes and cute dimples when she smiled, Mary became aware that Dr. Powell was a very attractive lady and most definitely special to someone. She wondered why she hadn't noticed that before.

Dr. Powell said, "Ladies, I would like to get your input on something. I want to hypnotize Mary to find out what she's intentionally forgetting, and hopefully help her come to terms with all of this confusion she's feeling."

Mary looked at her sister. She nodded in approval. "How do you do that?" Mary asked the doctor.

"It's just like taking a nap. You've probably seen it on television, right?" Dr. Powell said.

"Yeah. They take a pocket watch and dangle it in front of the person and swing it back and forth till the person starts talking about stuff they remember from the past."

Dr. Powell answered, "Well, sort of. Only I don't use a pocket watch." She smiled and continued. "No, all I do is help you relax to the point where you can remember things. Sometimes we have so many distractions that we can't think clearly. All I do is help you concentrate on details, so that you can recall parts of your life that you need help remembering. Sound okay to you?"

"Yes, I think so."

"Do you want your sister to be present when we do this? It's totally up to you."

"It doesn't matter. If she wants to be here, then that's fine with me." Mary answered. She wanted Darlene there, but didn't want to make her feel obligated to stay. She was afraid she wouldn't remember what she said when she was under hypnosis, and she wanted to be able to ask Darlene about it later just in case. She hoped Darlene could be trusted.

Darlene thought for a moment before replying. "Yes, I would like to witness it. It won't interfere with anything if I'm here, right?"

"It shouldn't, but if it's an issue once we get started, we'll try it with Mary alone."

"When are we going to do this? I can come back whenever I need to." Darlene seemed to be anxious about the whole thing, which made Mary feel uneasy.

"That's up to Mary." Dr. Powell squatted next to Mary and put her hand on her knee. "We won't do anything until you're ready, okay?"

She considered the question for a moment. "Right now is fine. I'm afraid if I don't do it today, I might chicken out later. Dr. Powell, I think I can trust you, and I believe you can help me." She realized her palms were sweating, and she discreetly wiped them on her shirt.

With a surprised look, Dr. Powell said, "Okay, that's fine with me. Do you have time to stay today and go through this process with us?" the doctor asked Darlene.

Darlene shifted in her seat, took a deep breath and sighed. "Yep, now is as good a time as any."

Chapter 17

Mary knocked on the window of the car that Melanie was sitting in. Melanie didn't look up.

"Mel? Roll down your window. Open the door or something, okay?" Mary pleaded.

Melanie's mother, who was loading their belongings into the trunk of the car, didn't even acknowledge Mary.

"Why won't she talk to me?" Mary asked her.

Melanie's mother looked disgustedly at her without answering. Mary started crying, and leaned against the car. "Why won't anybody talk to me?"

"You're in my way," Melanie's mother said tersely as she brushed past Mary to place some clothing in the backseat of the car.

"But I really need to talk to her. You're moving away, and this might be the last time I see her. Please tell her. She'll listen to you."

Melanie's mother smiled tightly. In a sarcastic tone, she said, "Sure, I'll just tell her to get out of the car and talk to her best friend. You are her best friend, right?"

"I think I am."

"So why the hell didn't you watch out for her?"

Mary was shocked at the anger in the woman's voice. She was scared to say anything else, and just stared at her.

Melanie opened the car door and stepped out. "Follow me."

Mary trailed her friend to the small graveyard that was next to her house, waiting for some kind of explanation. She sat on a broken headstone, toppled over by a tree that had decided to grow in that very spot.

Sitting on the ground with her back against a big oak tree, Melanie said nothing for a while. Mary waited anxiously, watching her friend's face for a clue as to what she was thinking.

"My mother is going to be so mad that I came over here to talk to you," Melanie said, laughing a little. Her eyes were red and she looked downright sickly.

"I don't understand why y'all are so mad at me. What did I do?" Mary looked away from her friend, unable to handle her despondent appearance. She played with a leaf that had landed on her leg, twisting it around by its stem, studying its colors.

"You really don't know?" Melanie's voice was incredulous. She looked at Mary, her face flushed with emotion.

"All I know is that you're moving because your uncle got into trouble with the law, and your house is being taken away because some illegal stuff happened there."

"What the heck are you talking about?" Melanie sounded confused and looked hard at Mary.

"You know. . . the men with the turbans? The weapons and bombs that your uncle was selling and using your house to do it? All that stuff that went on." Mary wondered if her words sounded as bizarre to Melanie as they did to her.

"Men with turbans? Bombs and weapons? Oh God, you really are crazy, Mary." Melanie's tears made wet tracks down her face, and Mary fought the urge to wipe them away.

Closing her eyes tight, Mary tried to focus on her thoughts. She then looked at Melanie, who at this point seemed to be a different person to her. "You don't remember how we sat and laughed at dinner at all those crazy foreigners?" Mary's voice was pleading. She felt a desperate need for Melanie to validate something, anything she was saying.

"I have no idea what you're talking about. Nothing like that ever happened," Melanie said angrily. "Why would you make up something so weird?"

Mary stood up and backed away from her friend, nearly tripping over a small grave marker. She looked up to see a sign that said "Hill Cemetary". Mary's thoughts immediately went back to that evening when she was running from someone. "Wait a minute, what's going on here?" she said in a panicked voice.

"Mary, how dare you act like you don't know what's going on. After what your brother did to me. . ." Melanie stood up and looked at Mary with such hatred, she felt as if her friend might even hit her.

"Huh?"

"He raped me! Your bastard brother raped me! He may as well have shit on me — it was awful, and you know that's why we're moving!" Melanie sobbed into her hands.

Mary felt like she had been punched in the stomach. She walked over to her friend to comfort her. As she reached for Melanie's hand, it was slapped away by Melanie's mother, who had arrived unnoticed by either of the girls. Mary withdrew her hand as if it had been burned.

The two stared at each other for a moment. Melanie's mother's eyes were fierce. Mary finally gave in and looked away, partly out of respect and partly out of fear. She bowed her head and looked at the ground.

"Don't you touch her. It's because of you and your trashy family that we have to move. Your mother and father are terrible parents, letting you kids go into bars, letting you dance with men. No wonder none of you are turning out to be worth anything. I pity you kids because you never had a chance!"

Mary said nothing. She felt like she had just been beaten. She knew that Melanie's mother had spoken the truth. It was as if she had said out loud what everyone in town must be thinking. Still, the humiliation of her words paled in comparison to the sadness she felt for her friend.

Melanie's mother put her arm around her daughter, who seemed to have calmed down somewhat. Melanie buried her face in her mother's shoulder, refusing to look at Mary. Besides her sniffing from crying, Melanie was quiet. Mary wished that she would say something. Even something spoken in anger would be better than the silent treatment.

Mary watched her best friend walk away with her mother. Their loathing of her was painfully clear. "I'm so sorry. I don't want you to go!" she sobbed. She knew there was nothing she could say that would make any difference. She imagined Dee pawing at her friend, and the thought made her sick. *Somehow he manages to mess up everything.*

Melanie and her mother got into their car and started driving away. Mary felt betrayed by Dee, and sorry right down to her core. It was because of their friendship that Melanie had been hurt. She waved, hoping Melanie would see her and know that she loved her dearly. She didn't see her look back, but waved until the car was out of sight, just in case.

Mary got up and started walking back home. *Why wouldn't she have told me?* Mary wondered. *We're so close. . . we've never had any secrets from each other.* Nothing made sense to Mary anymore.

Glancing back at the cemetery, she thought about that night that someone was after her, and she ran through the graveyard and into the old tobacco barn. It seemed like a dream now. *That did happen, didn't it?* she asked herself. A dull ache settled in Mary's chest as she realized that her memories had somehow become distorted.

How could I have imagined a whole story about Melanie's uncle selling weapons and all those Arabs? I've never even seen people like that, and yet I can remember exactly what they were wearing, how they talked, and the way they acted. . . Mary tried to recall if she had seen something like that on television or in a movie, or maybe even read about it at school, and then maybe imagined it to be true. She shook her head. *No, I know those things happened.*

A foreign man kissing her hand, the sound of Melanie's laughter, running through the graveyard, the smell of the barn — they all flashed vividly through Mary's mind as she lay in bed that night.

Trying to make sense of it all, she stared at the ceiling. Outside, she heard crickets chirping and smiled a little thinking about Doc calling her "Trichet". *For all I know, I imagined that, too.*

Unable to sleep, Mary sat up in bed and looked out the window. She made a wish on a star that she would see her friend again someday.

She also wished that her brother was dead.

Chapter 18

"You're going to feel very sleepy and comfortable, Mary. You're safe here. Just relax, and concentrate on what I'm saying."

Mary nodded, and looked at her sister. Darlene seemed concerned, and focused intently on the doctor's instructions to her sister. She looked like she didn't know what to do with her hands as she fiddled with her purse, straightened her skirt, and fussed with her hair. She finally quieted her fidgeting hands by crossing her arms.

Mary turned her attention back to Dr. Powell, who said, "Okay, Mary, you're thinking back to a time when you were a child. You are a young girl, and you are living with your mother and father. Do you see that?"

"I do, but you know what? I'm not really asleep." She looked at the doctor ruefully.

"That's okay. Just stay with me here. Go ahead and close your eyes, and tell me what you're thinking. Do you see your parents?"

Mary's eyes slowly closed. For a moment, she was quiet, then softly she answered, "Yes."

"Do you see the rest of your family, too?"

Mary frowned. "Yes."

"Who do you see?"

"Dr. Powell, I'm not really hypnotized. I'm not really asleep."

"That's okay. Just concentrate. And tell me who you see when you think of your family."

"I see my mother, father, sister and brother."

"Okay."

"I hate my brother Dee."

"Why?"

"He's mean."

"Tell me what he's doing."

"He hurts everybody that comes around."

"Who does he hurt, Mary?"

"Everybody."

Dr. Powell looked at Darlene, who seemed captivated by Mary's recollection of her brother. "So, what happened to him?" the doctor asked.

"I don't know."

"Think. Just take your time. Do you remember the last time you saw him?"

"There was a car wreck. It was really bad."

The doctor wrote notes as she listened. "Okay, and what happened?"

Darlene listened closely, nervously playing with her purse handle. She crossed and uncrossed her legs. Dr. Powell looked at her as if to tell her to be still. She made an apologetic face and mouthed "sorry" to the doctor.

"We left the bar, and my brother was too drunk to drive, so my father drove. He was also too drunk to drive, but my brother was sick, so. . ."

Darlene dug a tissue out of her purse. Tears welled up in her eyes as she listened.

"We ran off the road and over a bridge. When I woke up, I was a good ways from the car. It was laying on its side. I was hurting in my chest, but I crawled over to see if my parents were okay."

"What did you see?"

"They looked like they were dead. They were all bloody and laying in weird positions. It was so scary!" Mary started breathing hard, and winced as if she were reliving the scene.

"Remember, you're safe here. We're just looking back and remembering. Nothing can hurt you now."

Mary licked her lips and her eyes fluttered. "I figured they were dead, so I crawled over to see my brother. His body was sort of halfway in the car -- his legs were still in the car, and his shoulders and head were laying on the ground. But he was alive. He was moaning."

"What happened next?"

"Well, I hated his moaning. I hated him. He was so mean. He hurt everybody I loved." Mary paused to take a deep breath. "So I picked up the biggest rock I could find and I busted his head."

Darlene cried loudly, and a wide-eyed Dr. Powell motioned for her to leave the room.

"Okay. So you hit him on the head with a rock." The doctor spoke slowly and deliberately. "Mary, you're remembering important things now. What happened next?"

"I was barely able to walk," Mary continued, "so I don't even know how I picked up that rock, but I did, and it killed him when I did that. At least that's what I thought at the time." Mary peeked at the doctor and saw her making an awful face. "I was glad I killed him. He deserved it."

"Why did he deserve it? Why do you think Dee was so bad?"

Mary said flatly, "He was the reason I lost my boyfriend, my parents, and my best friend Melanie. He really was an awful person."

Dr. Powell took a deep breath. "I'm going to bring you out of hypnosis now. You will remember what we talked about, but you won't be upset about it or dwell on it. You're warm and safe as you wake up. I'm with you, and you're okay."

Mary opened her eyes and looked at the doctor. "I really did kill my brother, didn't I?" A tear ran down her face. "Am I going to jail?"

"No, honey, you're not going to jail. For one thing, I have to keep anything we talk about confidential. For another, there's no way you can be absolutely sure you killed Dee. Maybe you just think you did. The only reason we're even talking about it now is because you need help dealing with what happened."

Mary sat up on the couch and took a deep breath. "I really would like to just go back to my room and be by myself for a while."

Dr. Powell called in a nurse and had Mary escorted back to her room. "And if you see her sister in the hallway, please have her come back and see me, okay?" she said to the nurse.

Mary walked into her room and sat on the edge of her bed. Her head hurt, and she was more tired than she had ever remembered. As she began to lie down and close her eyes, she realized she hadn't even told her sister goodbye. She quickly walked out of her room and back toward the doctor's office, praying that the nurse wouldn't see her.

Upon reaching the doctor's office, she saw that her sister and the doctor were having a conversation. Instead of interrupting them, she watched and listened through the cracked door.

"Thank you for coming back in to talk to me. I was afraid you had gone home," Dr. Powell said, as Darlene sat down in the chair in front of her desk.

"Oh, I wouldn't have left. I want to help Mary get better. I want to help in any way I can."

"Well, evidently Mary can remember events clearly when she's hypnotized. Otherwise, it seems that the way she copes with tragic events in her life is to dream up grandiose, sometimes totally inaccurate versions of what happened. Your sister is seriously disturbed. The fact that she hated your brother so badly comes out in the fantasies she has about him. She's told me that he murdered your parents by strangling your mother with a rope and dumping her by the creek, and she said that he decapitated Robert and fed his body to the pigs."

Darlene gasped. "She told you that?"

Dr. Powell nodded. "Not during hypnosis, but in other therapy sessions. When she's under hypnosis, she tells the truth about how things happened."

"But she says she's not really hypnotized."

"I understand that, but she *is* very relaxed and she's at least able to discern real events from imaginary ones. She blames Dee for all the bad things that happened in her life, so she manipulates her dreams around the hatred that she felt for him. In other words, in a roundabout way, she feels like he's responsible for your parents' deaths, so to her, the story in her head about him murdering them seems very real and plausible. She relates the details quite vividly.

"Another situation is her friend Melanie. It hurt her so badly to think of Dee hurting her best friend that she fabricated some wild story in her mind about Melanie moving away because of something her uncle did. It's a coping mechanism," Dr. Powell explained.

"So she really doesn't know what's real and what isn't," responded Darlene. "Like that Doc character she talked about. I never knew anyone like that."

The doctor nodded. "Basically, she lives in a fantasy world. She weaves truth and fiction together, and somehow makes it all combine to explain away things that are tormenting her. I think that sometimes she totally believes what she's dreamed up, and then the next day she makes up something else. At times, the bad stuff bubbles to the surface, and she has horrific images of things that never happened. Other times, she invents off-the-wall stories that cover up bad things that really did happen."

Darlene stared blankly at the doctor.

"It's like she scrubs and sanitizes a situation when she can't deal with it, and other times she gives in and allows herself to feel the pain, but she distorts it to the highest, most shocking level. It's all skewed, and she can't seem to make heads or tails of it. In other words, she doesn't know how to handle her own feelings without an internal struggle."

"Is she ever going to be well enough to come home?" Darlene asked.

"As long as she doesn't pose a threat to herself or anyone else, I think it's a possibility. Right now, though, she's better off here. We have a lot of work to do. There are many things going on in her head that need to be addressed. She has a hard time accepting the fact that she's an adult. It's like she's in a time warp. She needs some help getting out of it."

Darlene let the doctor's words settle before answering. "Should I just keep coming to visit her then?"

"Absolutely. You are a good sister and the best friend she's got. It'll help, you being here for her."

"I do have one more question, though. Who is this Melanie you keep talking about?"

In the hallway, Mary closed her eyes and leaned against the wall for support. *I really am losing my mind. . . Maybe I've lost it already.*

Chapter 19

Mary's parents' funeral took place on an unusually warm fall day. Two gravesites, side-by-side had been dug, and Robert and Judy's caskets were suspended on lowering mechanisms above their perspective resting places.

Geese honked overhead as they traveled south for the winter. Mary wished that she was flying with them. She sat in one of the folding chairs that were placed on fake green grass-like carpeting next to the gravesites.

"Honey, are you still sore from that car wreck?" asked a woman Mary didn't recognize who seemed to come out of nowhere.

"Yes ma'am. My neck hurts, and I didn't sleep too good last night."

The woman gingerly squeezed Mary's shoulder, and smiled sympathetically at her. "I'm so sorry about your mama and daddy, and your brother, too, of course. They're going to have his funeral tomorrow, right?"

"Yes, ma'am."

The woman turned to a man standing next to her and whispered, "It's got to be hard to bury your mama and your daddy on the same day."

The man shook his head. "Poor little thing."

Mary wished Melanie was there. Everything was better when she was around.

She looked up to see dozens of friends, neighbors and family members stealing glances at her. *If they only knew that I'm the reason they're going to be burying Dee tomorrow, they wouldn't be so nice to me*, Mary thought.

Mary looked at the ground and thought about how cold it must be in the winter, and what happens to the caskets underground when it rains. She wondered if they were really water-tight, or if they leaked. She suspected they leaked. Eventually.

While contemplating the deterioration process of dead bodies after they're buried, Mary felt the pressure of a hand on her shoulder. Assuming it was her sister, she patted the hand and rested her cheek against it.

"Are you okay?" a man's voice said.

Mary looked up to see Devin standing there. She felt breathless as she struggled for something to say.

Devin sat in a chair next to Mary and took her hand. "I've been worried about you ever since I heard about the car crash. I'm so glad you weren't hurt too badly."

The look of concern on Devin's face overwhelmed Mary, and she leaned into him and cried. He patted her back, then gently pushed her away. He looked around as if he were afraid people would see them. Mary suddenly felt conspicuous and stifled her display of emotion.

"Yes, I'm okay," she murmured, "but I'm sore all over. It hurts to get in and out of bed, and even right now my neck is hurting." She looked at the handkerchief in the pocket of his suit, purposely taking her attention off his handsome face.

"I just can't believe this happened. You let me know if there's anything I can do for y'all, you hear?" he said, almost whispering it to her.

Mary nodded.

"I'll see you tomorrow at your brother's funeral, okay?"

"Okay."

Devin got up and walked to the back of the crowd. He began a conversation with a man who was dabbing his eyes with tissue. Mary had no idea who the man was until she realized that it was the guy who had wanted to hug her that day at the pig pen. He was wearing a suit, and he looked a lot different than she remembered, but he still had those beady eyes. She turned around quickly so he wouldn't see her.

She looked back at Devin several times as he walked through the crowd of mourners, disappointed that he didn't meet her gaze. She almost felt worse about the way he treated her than about anything else that was going on. She wondered if he'd ever cared about her in the first place as she forced herself to face forward, fighting the urge to look back at him again.

Mary decided that she wouldn't go to Dee's funeral the next day. She had a headache from crying, and she wondered if it was possible to have a crying hangover. If there was such a thing, she felt like she had it. Besides, if Devin was acting too ashamed to talk to her, she didn't want to give him the opportunity to be so uncaring again. And why should she go anyway? She was glad her brother was dead. She shivered and pulled her sweater tight around her shoulders.

The funeral seemed to go slowly to Mary. Her mind wandered, and she pretended that the people that were being buried were not her parents. These people could be anybody. *I don't have to admit who they really are, do I?*

Then she imagined that her parents weren't really dead at all and that all of this was a dream. She fantasized that when she got home, her mother would be cooking supper and that her father would be working on something in the barn. And when she went to the barn to see what he was doing, the baby pigs would be oinking at her to feed them some wild green onions.

Chester would be walking behind her, then he would run off into the field to chase a rabbit. . . zigzagging frantically, all that would be visible of him was his white tail sticking up above the tall grass, wagging excitedly. She would hear him bark, with his unmistakable half-bark, half-howl, elated at the scent of the rabbit. She smiled at the thought.

The preacher finished up his graveside prayer and people began to disperse, hugging each other and saying their final goodbyes to Robert and Judy. Some stood in respectful silence, looking on as the caskets were lowered into the holes in the ground. Most people stopped by to give a kind word to Mary and her sister. *The worst of it is finally over*, Mary thought.

Exhausted, Mary returned home with Darlene and went straight to bed. She tried to sleep, pulling the covers all the way over her head to block out the light of day. But all she could picture when she closed her eyes was her brother moaning in pain before she smashed the rock down on his head. She closed her eyes tight and smacked her forehead with her hand, trying to erase the image.

Before long Darlene came into her room and sat at the foot of the bed. "How do you feel?"

Pulling the covers down so she could see her sister, Mary could tell she had been crying. She had dark circles under her eyes. She pulled a tissue from her pocket and blew her nose. Then she looked back at Mary, waiting for a response.

"I'm okay, I think."

"You'll feel better in a few days. I had a wreck once, and I was sore for two weeks."

"I feel guilty," Mary said.

"Guilty for what?" Taken aback, Darlene stared at her.

"I don't know. . ." Mary hesitated.

With a sigh of exhaustion, Darlene said, "If there's something on your mind, you may as well talk to me about it. All we have is each other now."

Mary nodded. "I guess I just feel guilty that everyone else in the car died and I lived." She sat up in the bed, putting her pillow behind her for support as she leaned back against the headboard.

"Don't feel guilty. Be thankful. You have nothing to feel bad about." Darlene looked like she was tired of the conversation.

"But you don't understand. I really need to tell you something." Putting her hand on her sister's arm, Mary looked directly into her eyes.

Darlene flinched subtly and patted Mary's hand. "Shh. No, I don't want to hear anything right now. I don't think I can take any more."

"But you don't even know what I'm going to say. I mean, I really need to get something off my chest. This is something you need to hear."

Darlene shook her head. "No, I don't think I want to go into all of that right now."

"But you asked." Mary felt like her disappointment had filled the room.

"I know. But please. Just rest, and we can talk later." Darlene stood up and walked slowly toward the door. "I'm going to go lay down, too. I'm so worn-out."

Chapter 20

"Yeah, you can say something, but nobody will believe you," he said as he zipped up his pants. "You're stupid and ugly, and nobody cares about a thing you say." He spit on the ground and looked down at Mary with a disgusted look on his face. He wiped his mouth with his sleeve and turned his back to her.

Mary rolled over onto her side. It took all of her strength to sit up. She took a deep breath, reflecting on what had just happened. She clumsily kicked a tobacco stalk that was lying on the barn floor as she scooted herself into an upright position. Her legs felt weak as she made a quick assessment of herself.

"Hurry up and get back home before Mama and Robert get there," Dee said as he tightened his belt around his waist. He was in such a hurry his hands were shaking.

"I'm going to tell Daddy about this," Mary whispered. She tried to control her emotions, her chin quivering. Tears threatened to fall, but she wiped them away before they streamed down her face.

"'I'm going to tell Daddy about this,'" Dee mocked. "Oh yeah? Well, go ahead. Mama won't let him do anything to me. You'll see," he said condescendingly before turning his back to her again.

The arrogant look on his face was more than Mary could stand. Now that it was all over, it was interesting to her that he didn't even want to look at her — like she was revolting to him. Only minutes before, his uncontrollable desire to dominate her seemed all-consuming. *How can it be that way? How can a person do the most intimate thing with you, and then turn around and be so mean?*

Mary managed to get on her feet, brushing away the dirt and bits of hay that were clinging to her skin. She picked up her clothes that had been scattered on the barn floor, and hid behind a stall door to get dressed. A piercing ray of sunshine came through a crack in the barn, making a warm spot on her face. She shielded her eyes from the light with her hand. The intensity and brightness of it seemed inescapable. It felt like a spotlight on her bruised and humiliated soul.

The pain between her legs was a throbbing, raw feeling. She touched herself and saw blood on her hand. She had never seen that much blood before, and for a moment she wondered if she had been hurt badly. *Surely I'm not going to bleed to death,* she thought, feeling a little faint. Holding onto the stall door for support, she closed her eyes and willed herself to stay quiet. Screaming seemed unnecessary. No one would hear it anyway. Besides, she felt that there was no one who would come running to her defense. The hollow feeling of being all alone was almost unbearable.

Slowly she got dressed and stepped out from behind the stall door. Dee was looking at her with a sneer on his face. "Now, you know you ain't going to say anything about this, right?" He stared at her, waiting for an answer.

Mary didn't speak to him as she walked past him out of the barn. She felt like there was nothing left to say. To even acknowledge him was something he didn't deserve.

Grabbing her arm, Dee turned her around to face him. "Because, you know, you were smiling. You wanted it."

"I hate you. You're just a piece of shit!" Mary said, struggling against his grasp.

"Well, you might hate me, but you liked it." Dee grinned, and it made Mary want to slap his face. "I might have to tell ol' Devin about this."

"Don't you dare!" Mary said, starting to cry.

"Oh, yeah. He asked me one time, 'Did you ever poke her?' " Dee laughed evilly. "He did! And now I can tell him I sure did."

"You are LYING!" Mary screamed into his face. She began hitting him with all the strength she could gather, scratching any uncovered surface of skin with her fingernails.

He laughed. "You can't hurt me." His eyes weren't laughing, though. They were focused on her, mocking her weakness.

"You asshole!" Mary screamed as she realized that he had both of her wrists in one hand. Her brother was so much stronger than her, and all the desperate fighting she could do would never be a match for him. He was amused at her feeble attempt to get away from him.

Mary considered spitting in his face, but instead she yelled, "Your daddy won't even claim you! Mama said that he won't even say that you're his kid!" She tried to writhe out of his grasp, but it was no use.

Momentarily, Dee stared at her with his teeth clenched. They were poised inches away from each other in a standoff of sorts. She knew that for once, she had hit a nerve. His eyes narrowed as the hate that he felt for her seemed to ooze out of him. "He does so admit that I'm his son." He let go of her wrists and backed slowly away from her.

"No, he doesn't. He admits that our sister is his daughter, but he doesn't want YOU!" she said spitefully. "I guess you're lucky my father took you in to raise. He hates you, though. Really, he just looks at you as the bastard that you are."

With a subtle smile, Dee looked at her and appeared to be sizing her up. "I could bury your ass alive, you know that? Right here, right now. I could snap your boney little neck and throw you in a hole in the ground."

"Go ahead." Mary said. She felt like she meant it. Her whole life seemed to be worthless at that moment.

Dee leaned back on the side of the barn and looked at the ground. "So, we have a deal. If you breathe one word of this, I'll tell Devin. And that's the bottom line." He looked at her hard for a few seconds, letting his words sink in.

Mary looked back at him without answering. He knew that she wouldn't say anything. No matter what, she didn't want Devin to know what had happened. She was ashamed and somehow felt like it was her own fault for always being alone and vulnerable. *I'm an easy target,* she thought to herself as she stood in the entrance of the barn and watched her brother walk away. His confidence that she would say nothing infuriated her. The bitterness of it consumed her.

As Mary walked home, she picked her way through a cemetery, noting that most of the headstones had the name "Hill" on them. She stopped to sit on one of the tombstones. Her legs were weak and she felt sick and empty. Tears came to her eyes as she thought about what her brother had told her. Did Devin really say those words "did you ever poke her?" That was so nasty. *No, he wouldn't say something disrespectful like that.*

Mary looked up at the blue sky, which was starting to fade as evening drew near. Her body was hurting. Her mind was hurting. And yet she felt numb.

The words echoed in her head. . . *poke her, poke her, poke her.* Mary put her hands over her ears to make the sound of Devin's voice go away. He would never say something like that –- not about her.

After what seemed to be an eternity or maybe only a few minutes, Mary decided to walk home. The sun was beginning go down, and Mary walked carefully toward her house. More than anything, she was afraid she would step on a snake. She deliberately scooted her feet as she walked, figuring she would scare off anything that wanted to bite her. *Wouldn't that be adding insult to injury,* she thought, *to be bitten by a fucking snake on top of everything else?*

As usual, the house seemed deserted as she stepped up on the concrete front porch. A cat was sprawled out on it, yawning with boredom. Moths were flying around a single light bulb that lit up the front porch. Mary quickly opened the door, hurried inside, and closed it behind her so they wouldn't fly into the house. She laughed at herself. *Who gives a shit if a few moths come into this house?*

She went to her room and went to bed, still dressed in the clothes she'd worn that day. She told herself that she would throw them away the next morning. Hearing the front door slam, she assumed her brother was home. She realized she wasn't afraid as she turned over to go to sleep. *What could he do that's worse than what he already did to me today?*

Chapter 21

"Come turn the water on for me," Judy said, leaning her head over the sink. "I've got dye all over my hands."

Mary turned the water on for her mother, careful of the brown hair color that not only covered her mother's head, but her hands and neck. She watched while her mother rinsed it out and handed her a faded maroon towel that was laying on the counter when she was done. "Here," she said shoving the towel into her mother's hand as she reached blindly for it.

"Oh, thanks." As she stood straight, she wrapped the towel around her head like a turban.

"Want me to get your camel?" Mary said, laughing. She hated fake laughing, and here she was, doing that very thing.

"Ha ha, you are so funny!" Judy said, grinning at her daughter. She sat down on a chair next to the sink and lit a cigarette.

Mary hesitated a moment before speaking. "Mama?"

"What?" Judy said, taking a long drag off her cigarette. She reached over to get an ashtray that was sitting on the edge of the kitchen table.

Mary waited a moment and continued. "I wanted to talk to you about something." Not knowing which direction the conversation would go, she decided to be selective about the words she used. No need to blurt everything out at once.

Judy seemed to understand that Mary had something serious to say. She looked at her daughter in anticipation, absentmindedly tapping the ashes off her cigarette. She was biting the inside of her cheek, a sign that Mary recognized as a nervous habit of her mother's. "Go ahead."

Mary sat in the farthest chair from her mother. She crossed her legs and hesitated. She wasn't sure how to begin. "What if I told you that somebody hurt me?"

The cigarette in Judy's hand was smoldering as she looked through the spirals of smoke at Mary. She grimaced and said, "What?"

Mary wanted to get up and say nevermind, but she sat still, hoping that the right words would come to her. They didn't. She sat silently and twisted a loose button on her shirt.

"What's this all about?" Judy prompted. She put her cigarette out in the ashtray and waved the lingering smoke away with her hand.

"Well. Somebody hurt me, and I think I need to tell you about it."

Judy stood up and walked toward her daughter. The towel on her head had shifted a little, revealing some dye that had collected around her ear. Mary wanted to reach up and wipe it off.

As Judy leaned toward Mary, she said softly, "You can tell me. Who hurt you?" She took Mary's trembling hand in hers and held it.

The gentleness of her mother and the kindness in her voice made Mary cry. "I don't know how to tell you."

"It's not your daddy, is it?"

"No, oh no!" Mary said insistently. The need to protect her father from such an accusation made the words nearly explode from her mouth.

"Is it. . . is it your brother?" Judy asked, closing her eyes as if she couldn't bear the answer that she knew was coming.

Mary nodded and looked away from her mother.

"Have you told your daddy?"

"No."

"Don't. He'd kill him."

Mary cried and held her mother's hand tightly. She was afraid if she let go, even if she loosened her grip, her mother would change her mind and leave her helplessly abandoned in her sorrow. "Please make him leave me alone," Mary said softly, her voice barely above a whisper.

Suddenly, her mother pulled away as if she had touched something hot. A stern look came over her face as she spoke. "I want you to stay away from your brother."

Mary felt like she'd been slapped. "What? You're acting like it's my fault!" Mary said incredulously.

"I didn't say that. But you just need to stay away from him. That'll solve that."

The betrayal that Mary felt from her mother was crushing. *How can she be saying this to me? Why doesn't she go hurt him like he hurt me? Why won't she stand up for me?* "So that's it?" Mary asked. She was no longer crying. She was angry. Staring at her mother, she waited for a better answer.

"Yes, that's it. That's all you can do. I mean, I'm sorry that happened to you, but sometimes that's what happens when you have girls and boys in the same house." Judy paused for a minute before continuing, "I mean, what is it that you want me to do about it?" Judy's deadpan tone sounded unbelievably cold and uncaring to Mary. And her response was irrational.

Judy lit another cigarette and finished cooking dinner. Mary watched her set the table as if their conversation had never taken place. "Get some forks out, would you?" Judy said.

As Mary collected the utensils to set on the table, she grasped a knife hard, pressing it into the palm of her hand, trying to physically match the stinging pain of her mother's disloyalty. A numbness was finally beckoned by Mary as she sat at the table and stared at the bowls of food her mother was placing on it.

Dee walked into the kitchen and stood behind his chair. A half-smile was on his face as he sat down and looked directly at Mary, almost daring her to say something to him. She was sickened by the cocky way he was acting and avoided looking at him. *He knows he's aggravating me,* Mary thought, *but I'm not going to give him the satisfaction of seeing me squirm.*

Robert walked into the room, drying his hands on a towel. "It's a hot one out there today," he said, draping the towel over the back of a chair. He sat down, and without waiting for anyone else, began dishing food onto his plate. "That garden needs some hoeing, so any volunteers would be welcome," he said looking up at Dee.

Shrugging, Dee reached for a biscuit and ignored Robert's comment altogether. Mary wondered how he always seemed to get away with his pompous attitude, like he thought he was the President or something.

"I'll take that as a no," Robert said, before taking a huge bite of corn.

As Judy sat down at the table, Dee pointed at her and busted out laughing. "You still have a towel wrapped around your head!"

Robert momentarily looked up from his plate and glanced at Judy. "Humph," he said and continued eating.

"Oops, I guess I do!" Judy laughed, stepping away from the table to pull it off. "There, is that better?"

"Sure." Dee acted like he was stifling laughter, but the phoniness of it was sickening, making him look silly and juvenile.

"Good. Start passing the food around, Mary," Judy said as she scooted her chair up to the table.

Dee smiled big and looked at Mary with satisfaction in his eyes. "Please pass the potatoes," he said to her, his blatant conceit evident. He was baiting her, and she knew it.

Judy shot a look of warning at Dee, but said nothing. Robert was shoveling food into his mouth and didn't seem to notice anything amiss whatsoever. He opened his mouth unnecessarily wide to take a bite out of a scallion, oblivious to how it looked to do that with a mouth full of food. Dee looked at his plate and pretended to concentrate on eating.

An awkward quietness fell over the room, in which the only noises to be heard were the clinking of the forks and knives against the plates. Occasionally, Robert's lips smacked, reminding Mary of the pigs eating at the trough. *He puts those pigs to shame,* she thought, watching her father gobble down his food like a starving field hand.

"Mama, these cathead biscuits are something else," Dee said as he helped himself to the last two on the plate. "They're gut bombs, but they sure do taste good."

"Put you some of that bulldog gravy on it," Robert said, food shrapnel shooting from his mouth as he spoke.

"Don't mind if I do," Dee said as he ate the rest of that, too.

The brazen carelessness of her family was maddening, and Mary's throat tightened with resentment. She didn't even try to drink any water for fear she would choke on it.

Chapter 22

"Okay, Mary. Go ahead and close your eyes. Remember how we did this before? I just want you to relax and let me know what you're thinking. Okay?"

Mary nodded.

"Okay. Where we left off is that your parents died in a car wreck and you hit your brother on the head with something."

"A big rock."

"Right. Now, we're going to move beyond that and talk about some things that happened before the wreck. Let's talk about you, Mary. What do you see when you look back at yourself? Tell me something you liked to do."

"I liked my animals." Mary smiled.

"Okay, that's a good start. Your animals meant a lot to you, didn't they? So, you spent lots of time with them."

"Yes, I liked my dog, and the cats were okay, too. I don't like cats as much as dogs, though."

"They were your friends, huh?"

"Yes. Besides a couple of girls I knew from school, they were my only friends."

"So, you've told me about a friend named Melanie before. Want to talk about her some more?"

Mary was quiet for a moment. Then she sat up and opened her eyes, looking directly at Dr. Powell. She searched the doctor's face for reassurance. The doctor gently but firmly guided her back down onto the couch.

"Okay, just be calm. There's no hurry on anything here. Just lie back down and think about something else. We won't discuss anything you're not ready to talk about."

Mary felt herself relax again as she rested her hands on her stomach. She breathed deep, feeling the support of her doctor wash over her. *This doctor can be trusted,* she thought. "Dr. Powell, I don't think I've told you everything about Melanie, have I?"

The doctor wrote notes in Mary's file. "You've mentioned her in our sessions, but I'm sure you haven't told me everything about her."

"I don't have anybody who cares about me at my house," Mary said, her voice sounding almost childish. "I'm all alone. And I need a friend so bad."

"Tell me about Melanie."

"Well, Melanie is a little younger than me. I wanted a friend I could sort of watch out for and keep bad things from happening to."

"That's a good thing to want."

"Yes, I thought so. Oh, Dr. Powell, I didn't do my job. I didn't protect her!"

"Now Mary, why is it your job to protect her?"

"Because I need somebody to protect me."

"Okay. Did you hear what you just said?"

"Yes, ma'am."

"Mary, Melanie is you."

"No, that's not true. She's my best friend."

"I know that's what you have said, but that doesn't mean that she's real. Think about it. And I asked your sister, and she doesn't remember Melanie."

"My sister was hardly ever around, you know. She stayed with her daddy most of the time. She's a lot older than me."

"I realize that, but Mary, she was around sometimes, right?"

"Yes."

"Let's talk about the day your brother hurt you."

"I'd rather not."

The doctor sighed and answered, "Okay, I won't push you, but as soon as you're ready, we really do have to talk about it."

Mary readjusted the pillow under her neck and put her hands to her side. The doctor waited a moment before continuing, "Do you want to discuss this another time? Is there something else you'd like to talk about?"

"It wasn't in our barn, it was in a barn down the street where they hang tobacco."

The doctor listened, writing in Mary's file. "Why were you in a different barn?"

"I go walking all the time to get away from the house. I hate it there. There are barns everywhere out there in the country. Anyway, I guess he must've followed me."

"Okay, so you're walking down the street and you decide to go into the other barn?"

"Yes. I had to walk through a graveyard to get to it, but I liked that old barn and I wanted to see it."

"Did you know your brother was following you?"

Mary pressed her lips together. The doctor noticed perspiration on her face. "Are you okay?"

"Yes."

"So, did you know he was following you?"

"Yes."

"Did you try to get away from him?"

"No."

"Why didn't you just turn around and go home?"

"I wanted to play a game."

"What kind of game?"

"I knew what he wanted, so I played the game where I tease him and then I run."

"So, you had done this before?"

"Yes. But he never chased me down before."

"But this time?"

"This time he caught me, and when he did, he pushed me onto the ground in the barn."

"And that's when he had sex with you?"

"Yes."

"Were you scared?" Dr. Powell looked at the clock. It had been nearly an hour since they'd first started.

"Yes, I was, because I didn't know what he was going to do to me. And it hurt." Mary began to cry. "And Dr. Powell, it was all my fault because I knew what I was doing and I didn't stop him before it went too far!"

"No, Mary, it is NOT your fault. You are never to blame, do you hear me?"

Mary nodded and cried. "I'm a terrible person — a very bad girl."

"No, you're not bad. You are a nice girl, and you didn't do anything that made him hurt you. He did that all on his own." Dr. Powell put Mary's file on her desk and said, "Okay, I think you need a break from this. I'm going to bring you out of your hypnosis now. We've covered a lot today. Are you ready to wake up and talk?"

"Yes, ma'am. By the way, I'm not really asleep."

Dr. Powell laughed softly. "I know that. But you're relaxed, so I just say that you're asleep. You know what I mean. Go ahead and open your eyes."

Mary's eyes opened and she focused on the doctor. "I know you said that you don't think I'm a bad person. But I really need to know — do you think I'm crazy?"

"No, of course not."

Mary paused, "I have some other stuff I'd like to talk about with you. If you have time, that is."

"Sure I do. What else would you like to talk about?"

"Devin."

"You've mentioned him before. Mary, is Devin a real person?"

"Yes."

"Tell me about him."

"A man named Devin used to come into the bar that my parents ran. Devin Hill. I had a big crush on him. Actually, I think I loved him, and I'm pretty sure he loved me, too."

"But he was an adult and you were a child, right?"

"Yeah, that's true. But all that didn't matter. I saw the way he looked at me. Yes, he loved me, too. I know it."

"Okay, so what happened with Devin?"

Chapter 23

Mary was as happy as she could ever remember when Devin pulled her close and kissed her on her forehead. He casually moved his hands up and down her back, sending waves of excitement all over her body.

"I never thought about meeting in a graveyard before," Devin laughed. "It's pretty funny that you would pick a place like this to talk." He pointed to the corner of the graveyard. "My granny is buried right over there."

Mary was nervous as she sat on an overturned tombstone. She looked at her hands and wondered if Devin knew how anxious she was. "I'm actually kind of surprised that you agreed to come here and talk to me," she said.

"Are you kidding me? Of course I would."

"But remember what you said, I'm just a kid." Mary looked up at him momentarily, then shifted her gaze back to the ground. She wondered what he was thinking.

"I have a confession to make, Mary."

"You do?"

"You know that night when you got a call from a stranger?"

"Uh, yeah, it scared me half to death."

Smiling in spite of himself, Devin replied, "That was me."

Mary looked at him with surprise. "It was?"

"Yes. I figured your parents left you at home that night, and I wanted them to bring you there to be with me. So, I faked the whole thing. I called your house from a pay phone at the store across the street from the bar. Are you mad at me?"

Mary stared at him, her stomach tight. "I don't know. I mean, I don't guess so," she stammered. "You did that to be with me?" It seemed silly to her that he would go through that charade to see her. All he had to do was ask.

Devin took Mary's hands in his and pulled her up to face him. He put his arms around her waist. "Yes." His voice was thick with desire, which he seemed to be fighting to control. She could feel his body tremble, and all she wanted at that moment was to give herself to him, whatever that meant. She didn't care about his crazy prank. On the contrary, right now it seemed flattering to her, even if at the time it had seemed scary.

Devin reluctantly took his hands off Mary. Stepping back to lean against a tree, he looked at her anxiously. He seemed nervous as he picked little bits of bark off the tree and let them fall to the ground.

"But when you said I was just a kid, I thought you meant that you didn't think of me like that," she said.

"I'm not exactly an old man myself. I just turned twenty-one not too long ago. In a few years, it won't seem like I'm much older than you at all."

Mary smiled at him. He said "in a few years". *He must really like me if he's thinking about us being together in the future.* Taking a deep breath, she decided she would say what was on her mind.

"I wondered if you had a girlfriend."

Devin laughed. "I have a couple of them, yes."

Mary stared at him with her mouth open.

"Better close your mouth, girl!" Devin sniggered at Mary's response. "I was only kidding. I had a girlfriend for a while, but she got pregnant by another guy. So, what can I say? I had to turn her loose."

"Did you really love her?"

Devin paused for a moment, "Nah, not really. She was a big ol' girl. Too fat for me." Extending his arms wide, he made a face and shook his head. "Ugly, too. Cut her hair real short, like a dyke. I really don't want somebody like that. I want somebody little and cute like you."

"Oh." Mary managed to say, her face feeling flushed. *Good God, he's more immature than I am*, Mary thought.

"Yeah, it was weird. She came to tell me she was pregnant, and I was like aw, man, I ain't ready for no baby. But then I didn't even have to say the words. She came right out and told me it wasn't mine. I was really relieved, let me tell you."

"Whose was it?"

"I don't know. But her brother told me that he scared the life out of the guy at the laundromat because he was a low-class fucker who wouldn't even admit he was the one that got her pregnant." Devin spit on the ground disgustedly. "Her brother knew that if I found out who it was, I'd probably have to go kick his ass."

Mary suddenly knew exactly who had gotten Devin's girlfriend pregnant. It was her own brother. "What if I told you I know who it is?"

"And how would you know?" Devin asked with an amused look on his face.

"I just do. So, what would you do to him?"

"Aw, I don't really care about that girl anyway, but I would like to know who the joker was that did that to her. Out of curiosity, that is."

"It was my brother Dee."

"Really. . .?" Devin looked dumbfounded. "Are you sure? Did he tell you that?"

"Yes, I'm sure. No, he didn't tell me, but I found out another way."

Devin frowned and then laughed sarcastically. "Well, I guess he did me a favor then, didn't he?"

The look on his face belied what he said, and Mary felt the need to take back what she had just told him. "If you didn't love her anyway, then why does it matter? I mean, who knows how many boyfriends she might've had?"

Looking at Mary with slight condescension, Devin answered, "It matters because. . . well, it just does. You might not understand stuff like this yet, Mary, but when a man is seeing a woman, it matters if she's true to him or not."

Mary felt like Devin was talking down to her, as if she was too young to understand anything. She decided to keep quiet and say nothing more about it. She felt stupid for her comments, and hoped he wouldn't hold them against her.

"So, have you ever had a boyfriend?" she heard him ask. She could feel the conversation going in another direction, and she didn't know how to navigate it. A rush of adrenaline made her feel as if she were in someone else's skin.

"No, I haven't. I mean, I've had boys at school who liked me, and some have even called me. But I've never had a real boyfriend."

"Have you ever even kissed a boy?" he asked, focusing on Mary's lips as he talked.

"Just once. At a rodeo. I was sitting on the tailgate of a truck, and a boy from school was walking by. And he just walked up and kissed me. Just like that! It really wasn't much of a kiss, now that I think about it."

Devin looked unimpressed by Mary's rodeo kiss confession as he stepped closer to her. He reached down and took her hands into his. As he pulled her to him, his lips parted slightly and he looked right into her eyes. *Oh God, this is it, he's finally going to kiss me*. The sun was shining behind him, right through his golden-brown hair, as she looked up and saw what she believed to be love in his eyes.

As Devin bent down to kiss her, Mary closed her eyes and smelled the scent of his face. He smelled like everything good, and she lingered with her cheek against his before slightly moving her lips toward his. The kiss was slow and gentle. Mary didn't stop to think about how to do it, like she had always thought she would; she was amazed at how intuitive it was. Devin's fingers ran along her face and down her neck, so soft it was almost imperceptible to her.

Devin pulled away and looked at Mary. He heaved forward and fell toward her. He had a look of surprise on his face as he reached his arms out to her. She reached out to steady him, then realized she was actually trying to catch him. Standing behind the spot where Devin had been kissing her was Dee. He was wringing his hand as if he had hurt himself by hitting Devin.

Moaning with pain, Devin attempted to roll over onto his side. He then seemed to pass out; there was no more movement from him as he lay there, his face covered with mud from falling face first into the soft ground. Mary looked at her brother, who seemed to be oblivious to her standing there.

Dee wiped his forehead with the back of his hand as he studied what he had done. He leaned down to Devin's face and said, "Wouldn't it be ironic if you died in your own family's graveyard?" He stood up and looked at Mary, as if noticing for the first time that she was standing there. "So, what're you doing up here with him?" he asked with a scowl.

"What have you done? Look at him, you killed him!" Mary said, her voice no more than a squeaky whisper. She backed away from Dee, felt herself stumble, and knew she was going to fall. Her foot caught on the edge of a tombstone shaped like a harp, and she landed on her rear end on the ground.

"I saw his blue and white truck parked down there on the road and wondered what ol' Devin might be up to back here in this field. Well, now I guess we know, don't we?"

Devin moved a little and groaned. *Stay quiet*, Mary urged silently.

"Wait a minute, ain't you dead yet?" Dee said in a nasty tone. He put his foot on Devin's chest.

"Goddamn it, let me up!" Devin said breathlessly.

"Go on. Get up. And then get the hell out of here."

Devin struggled to get up. Mary was pushed back by her brother as she walked over to help him stand.

"Oh, no you don't. Let him get his own self up," said Dee. "And man, don't you come back here anymore, do you hear me?"

Devin stumbled out of the graveyard toward his truck without saying another word. He looked at Mary apologetically as he walked out of her sight. Mary heard his truck drive away and felt her heart go with him.

"Why is this any of your business anyway?" Mary turned to her brother and asked, tears running down her face.

"No, the question is, why are you seeing that guy? He's too old for you, and besides that, he screws every girl in town. You want to catch some kind of shit from him?"

"We didn't do anything."

"Yet."

"We just wanted to spend some time together, that's all!"

Dee studied her from head to toe. She didn't like the way he was looking at her, and she started to turn away.

"I guess Devin gets all the pussy, huh? Well, he missed out on this one this time." He smiled at Mary menacingly. Approaching her with a seductive look on his face, he reached out and touched her chest.

"I hate you!" screamed Mary as she began running. The only place she saw that she could go was a barn behind the graveyard. She began running toward it. Looking back, she saw that Dee was following behind her, but he didn't seem to be in a hurry as he deliberately made his way to the barn behind her. He was whistling, as if he was on his way to go fishing or something.

Chapter 24

"So what happened to Devin?" Dr. Powell asked.

Mary was glad that they were talking without the pretense of hypnosis. She wondered if she was ever really hypnotized. She never actually felt any different. At this point, things were starting to make more sense to her anyway. She sighed and answered, "I don't really know. He came to my parents' funeral, and then I never saw him again."

"Didn't he go to your brother's funeral, too?"

"I wouldn't know. I didn't go to it. He probably didn't, considering what had happened between them."

"I see."

Mary looked at the doctor, expecting more questions. The doctor was writing notes, occasionally looking up at her.

"Okay. So now what?" Mary asked Dr. Powell.

"That depends on you."

"Do you think I'm a sane person?"

Dr. Powell laughed. "You already asked me that. Of course I do."

"I wanted to hear it again from you," Mary said, only half jokingly.

"Okay, you are a sane person. And I think you feel better about yourself now, don't you?"

"Yes."

"And how do you feel overall? Physically, I mean."

"I feel fine."

"You look fine." Dr. Powell smiled. "You've been here for a few months now, and you have been very responsive to therapy. I feel that you really want to get on with your life. You've worked hard and put that defensive attitude of yours aside. That's been very helpful."

"I tried," Mary said.

"Your sister called and talked to me at length today."

"What did y'all talk about?"

The doctor took off her glasses. "You," she said.

"Well, I know that!" Mary said sarcastically.

"We talked about the possibility of you going home."

Mary waited for a moment before answering, "I would like that very much."

"Your sister sold the farm and has moved into an apartment. How do you feel about that?"

Mary thought about what the doctor said. She liked the idea that she never had to see that house again. *No point in having that place anymore*, she thought, *all the animals are long gone anyway.* "That's good. I don't like where I grew up. If I never see it again, I'll be happy."

"Good. And will you take your medications as I have prescribed?"

"Yes, ma'am," Mary answered.

"Alright, let's get on with it then. I still want to see you two times a week. I'll be giving you homework -- things to read, exercises to bring clarity to things we will cover in our therapy sessions, stuff like that."

"I promise to do anything that you ask me to do."

"Okay, I'll go ahead and let your sister know that she can come get you."

"Yes, please."

Dr. Powell smiled. "Mary, I'm very proud of you, and you are actually more normal than you think. We all try to escape reality by going off into our little dream worlds. It's just when you can't separate the two that it becomes a problem. You seem stable to me now, and as long as you don't have any setbacks, you probably will never have to come to stay in a place like this again." She stood up and walked around her desk, then took Mary's hand in hers.

"I guess this is goodbye then. For now," Mary said.

"As a resident, yes." Dr. Powell looked a little sad. "But we will be visiting with each other a lot in the future. I will be here for you no matter what, okay?"

"Yes, ma'am."

Happiness inspired Mary as she went back to her room to wait for her sister. Looking out the window, she saw a bright, sunny day awaiting her. Somehow it felt like she hadn't seen the sun that way before.

Mary used a box that someone had placed on her bed to pack her belongings. She didn't have anything to take with her except a jacket and a few books. Looking around the room that had been her home for a while, she was relieved that she wouldn't have to spend any more time there. The smell of it made her sick.

"Come on, girl!" Darlene said as she opened the door for Mary. "Let's get out of here. Want to grab something to eat on the way home? How about a chocolate shake?"

Mary laughed. "Yeah, that would be good." She was so excited about getting out of the hospital that food didn't even sound good to her, but she couldn't remember the last time she'd had anything sweet. Mmmm, chocolate; she could almost taste it.

They rode in silence for a while. Watching busy people driving around, walking the streets going here and there, Mary realized that the world had not stood still while she had been in the hospital. Somehow it did for her. People looked different to her, even though she had only been in the hospital for a few months. *Maybe it's me that's different*, Mary reasoned.

Darlene smiled reassuringly at her whenever she caught her eye. Smiles came easily for her now, and she responded in kind to her sister. She wished she had gotten to know her better. There was a sense of detachment there that Mary wanted to address. She figured it would work itself out as time went on.

"I have a surprise for you," Darlene announced with a sly grin.

Mary raised her eyebrows. "You do? What is it?"

"You'll see."

"Is it the apartment?"

"Well, in a way, yes, that's a surprise, too. You'll like it. There's a pool, tennis courts, a walking trail. Lots of stuff to do around there."

When they arrived at the apartment, Darlene said, "You open the door. Go ahead."

As Mary opened the door, she could hear whining and scratching noises. "What's that?" she asked.

"That's your surprise. Come with me."

Mary followed her sister to the laundry room, and in it was a dog crate with a puppy inside. She saw a little paw reaching through the crate opening. "Oh my gosh, what in the world?"

"It's your new dog! You can go ahead and let him out. He's all yours."

Mary lifted the puppy out of his cage and held him close to her. It was a baby hound dog, just like Chester. He licked her face and wiggled in an effort to get down and play. "I love him, thank you so much!" Mary jumped up and down and hugged her sister.

"Well, not only is he yours to love, but he's yours to clean up after, take for walks, feed. . ."

Mary rolled her eyes. "Well, I figured that."

Darlene laughed. "He sure is a sweet doggy. You know, the doctor said that this would be good for you, to have something to be responsible for."

"Thank you so much."

"So, what are you going to name him?"

Mary sat on the floor and let the puppy clumsily crawl up into her lap. She looked at him and thought for a moment. "He's small and cute, and he's such a helpless little thing," Mary said as she picked the dog up to look at his face. His eyes were bright as he looked back at her.

"Yeah, he's helpless now, but give him time. He's going to be a strong little guy," answered Darlene.

"Hmmm. . . I think I'll name him Cricket."

Chapter 25

Mary opened her eyes and sat up in bed. Yawning, she pushed the covers down toward the bottom of the bed with her feet. The mosquito bites that she had scratched like the dickens, leaving claw marks down her legs, were finally healing up a little.

"Mary!" Judy called, coming down the hallway. "Oh, you're up." She was standing at the door now. "What do you want for breakfast this morning?" She was wearing a housecoat, wiping her hands on a dish towel.

"Huh? Oh, sorry." Mary rubbed her eyes. "Pancakes?"

"Okay." Judy started to walk away from the door, then turned around and said to Mary, "Are you all right?"

"Yeah, why?"

"You just look like you don't feel too good this morning, that's all." She lingered at Mary's doorway, just in case there was anything else to be said.

A moment later, Mary looked up, and her mother was gone. Mary got out of bed and gazed at herself in the mirror. "I look fine," she said aloud. She pulled her hair back from her face, "Ooh, maybe she's right." Mary opened her mouth wide and looked at her throat. It looked normal to her, so she dismissed the idea of being sick. She was glad it was Saturday. At least she didn't have to hurry up to catch the school bus.

Mary quickly got dressed and combed her hair. It was probably dirty, but she decided she could go one more day without washing it. The well was dry again, and she'd have to heat some of the water on the stove to wash it. It hardly seemed worth the trouble.

As she walked down the hallway toward the kitchen, she could smell pancakes. It was a wonder to her that her mother was always willing to fix her whatever she wanted for breakfast. No matter how much the family lacked for food, somehow she was always able to come up with something good in the morning.

Judy put a plate of pancakes on the table in front of Mary and walked out of the room. After eating a few bites, Mary realized she wasn't as hungry as she had thought. Putting her plate in the sink, she noticed a pile of dirty dishes already sitting in it. "Mama? Whose turn is it to wash the dishes?" she asked loudly.

From somewhere in the house, "It's your brother's turn!"

Mary's brother walked into the kitchen and said, "Nope."

"Mama, he said he's not going to wash them!" Mary hollered to her mother, inches from her brother's face.

He smirked at Mary and blinked his eyes, mocking her.

"What?" Judy came into the room. "Oh, yes you will," she said to him.

"You mean heat up water on the stove and wash them damned dishes? No, uh-uh." He casually leaned against the counter and folded his arms.

Judy sighed. "Well, get out of here. Both of you. Hell, I'll just do them myself." She turned her back to them and they started to walk away. "And son. . .?"

Mary's brother turned to face Judy. "What?" he said, obviously annoyed.

"You need to start being nicer to everyone around here. You have to carry your load around this house just like everybody else."

"Yeah, yeah," he said, motioning with his hand as if he were jerking off.

Judy got in his face, seething, "And don't you ever, ever be disrespectful like that to me again. Do you hear me?"

He backed down from his mother and slunk away down the hall. Mary smiled, because for once, her mother not only stood up for herself, but she stood up for everyone else that her brother had treated so badly.

"What're you smiling about?" Judy turned to Mary.

"Oh, I was just. . . Uh, I mean, I don't know," she stammered.

"Humph, right. Well, you need to get off your high horse about it. After all, he *is* your brother."

"And what, I'm supposed to just love him unconditionally, as if I didn't know that he's mistreated me my whole life?"

"You don't have to love anybody. You don't even have to like him. But I don't want to hear you two bickering anymore."

Mary looked at her mother awkwardly.

Judy seemed to be challenging her with her eyes and posture. She looked back at her mother, unflinching.

Mary felt like her mother was daring her to say something. She decided to accept her mother's challenge. "Remember the day I told you that he hurt me?"

"What about it?"

"You didn't do the right thing." Mary's chest was heavy with dread at the thought of confronting her mother.

"And just what was I supposed to do?" Judy frowned at Mary.

"You should have held him responsible for the awful way he treated me. Don't you even care about me?"

"Of course I do!" Judy snapped.

"Then why didn't you punish him or make him apologize? Why didn't you fucking disown him?" Mary felt unusually brave as she demanded an answer from her mother.

"I don't know!" Judy yelled back. "You might ask yourself why you were even alone with him in the first place."

"What? Now it's my fault? I knew that's what you were getting at the first time I brought all of this up to you. You blame me, don't you?"

Judy lit a cigarette and sat in a kitchen chair next to the table. She inhaled the smoke deeply, and Mary could see her relax immediately. Looking out the back door, she seemed to be avoiding answering Mary's question.

"Well?" Mary demanded impatiently.

"No. Actually, I don't mean it that way. I don't blame you. I just blame the world for being the way it is."

"Huh? I think you would take the whole world's side before you'd take mine. That hurts, you know?" Mary felt tears running down her face, and realized that she was holding back a flood of emotions. She felt like they would've been wasted on this conversation anyway.

"I don't want to talk about this again. You hear me?" Judy pointed at Mary with the two fingers with which she was holding her cigarette. With a very serious look on her face, she stared at her daughter.

Mary took a deep breath. "Okay."

A cat on the porch pushed against the screen door, and the sound of it bumping the door frame made Judy jump. Mary studied her mother, who seemed so empty at that moment. She regretted the fact that she had said things that she knew would upset her. Especially when nothing could undo what had been done. She started to say something comforting to her mother, then Judy spoke.

"I want you kids to be happy. All of you deserve better than what you got. I take a big part of the responsibility for the fact that you didn't. But you've got to understand something. When I had your brother, I was all alone. I've always felt a special need to protect him."

"Protect him from. . . me?" Mary said, nearly whispering her question.

"From anybody. And I'm sorry, Mary. You've suffered a lot because of it." Judy watched her cigarette absentmindedly. "I'm really sorry I didn't do a better job of protecting you against him."

Mary felt relieved and wanted to put her arms around her mother, but she knew that she didn't like to be touched. It seemed to take a lot out of Judy to admit the way she felt.

Judy looked at her daughter with tears in her eyes. "See, what I didn't go into with you is that your brother has always had a mean streak in him. Ever since he was little. But I turned a blind eye to it. It was like I was sort of wrapped around his little finger. To me, even at his worst, he was still my innocent little boy. One day, when you have children, you'll know what I mean."

It seemed like a lame excuse to Mary, but then again she had to admit to herself that being a mother might very well make you feel that way. She still thought her mother's explanation was over-simplified, and her brother's actions definitely weren't justified.

"Besides, his daddy never would accept him as his own. I was the boy's mother and father, practically."

Mary nodded as if she understood.

"You okay now?" Judy asked, as if her explanations were sufficient enough to move on to some other subject.

"Yeah, I'm fine. And I'm sorry, too. Maybe I shouldn't have even told you that Dee hurt me."

"Dee?"

"Yeah?"

"Dee who?" Judy looked mystified. She stared at her daughter as if she were from another planet.

"My brother. . . Your son. . . Dee."

"Who calls him that?"

"We all call him that." Mary felt herself getting aggravated with her mother.

"Well, I never called him anything but Devin."

Mary looked hard at her mother. "No, Mama, not Devin. Dee is the one who hurt me. Devin wouldn't do that. I love Devin."

"I'm confused." Judy took a deep breath and let it out as a huge sigh, shaking her head.

"What's confusing about it?"

"Did you just say you love Devin? How? Like in what way?" Judy looked contemptuous, narrowing her eyes at her daughter.

Mary couldn't believe her mother was questioning her feelings. "Mama, you know I have a crush on him. You've known that since you and Daddy ran the bar."

"What in the world are you saying?"

"I love Devin, Mama. I am in love with him. And he loves me. Why can't you understand that?"

Judy recoiled at her daughter's declaration of love for Devin. She bit the inside of her cheek and sat looking at Mary, blinking. "Listen to me, Mary. Devin is your brother. And you cannot feel that way about him. It's unnatural."

"Devin is not my brother! Dee is!"

"Goddammit, there *is* no Dee!" Judy said firmly, smacking the kitchen table with her hand.

The strike of her mother's hand on the table startled Mary and she started crying again -- softly at first, then giving way to sobs that shook her whole body. "What are you telling me?" She took a deep breath, "Are you telling me that there is no Devin? Oh, God, please don't tell me that!"

"Yes, there's a Devin, girl! He's your brother!" Judy's angry voice echoed in the room.

"Well, Mama, my brother raped me in the fucking barn! And I know the difference between my asshole brother and the man I'm going to marry one day."

Judy stood up and wrapped her arms around Mary. It wasn't a warm embrace -- Mary knew her mother was trying to get control of the situation. She tried to shake her mother's hold but her arms felt like a steel trap. "Mary, honey, you need help. I'm ashamed of myself that I didn't get it for you sooner."

Robert walked in the front door, leaving it ajar as he stood and assessed the scene of his wife and daughter in what probably looked like a clumsy hug. "Uh, everything okay in here?"

Judy stood back from Mary and cleared her throat before answering, "Yes, everything's fine. Mary's fixin' to go take care of some chores is all."

Robert hesitated, "Okay. Well, Tootsie needs some corn thrown into her trough. I think all them babies she had is making her weary. Give her a bucket of water, too, all right? You can run out there and do that for me, can't you?" He didn't wait for an answer as he turned to walk out the door. "And you might want to do that pretty soon; I heard it's supposed to rain later today. Oh, by the way, some people are going to drop by tonight for a little get together."